A Once In A Lifetime Opportunity

A Novella By

Richard Webster

I

The Bar in Place Saint Georges

Jack Mears put his last fifty euro note on the counter and asked for a beer.

It was the fourth day in a row that he had come to this bar, which stood on the corner of a busy square in the old part of Toulouse. As on the preceding three days, he had arrived at the same time of two o'clock in the afternoon, and he would wait for precisely thirty minutes in case his associate from Marseilles showed up. And then he would leave, to return at the same time the following day.

And the day after that. And probably the next day too, until such a time as the meeting finally took place, or Jack gave up and moved on.

Jack's beer, the smallest measure they served, barely a thimbleful, was set down in front of him with his change – forty-six euros.

Leaving one euro as a tip, Jack scooped up the notes and put them in his pocket, next to the two twenties he knew to be there.

He now had eighty-five euros in his possession, plus the fifteen twenties hidden behind the wardrobe in his hotel room. Three hundred and eighty-five euros was the sum total of his wealth. It was everything he had in the whole world. A pathetic amount. Effectively zero, with an accounting error. A sum of money so small, so derisory, as to be worth nothing. And it was running out.

At least the hotel room was paid for until the end of the week, he told himself. It was a grim place, located in one of the worst parts of the city. But it was cheap, and the lock on the door worked, and the owner had offered him a deal for taking the room for a whole week.

So this week was covered but Jack knew that he couldn't stay on for a further one after that, as the cost of the hotel alone, seedy and decrepit though it was, would deplete his meagre resources to an unacceptable level. Even if he barely ate from now until then, and reduced his alcohol consumption to the one beer necessary to be able to wait in this bar for half an hour each day, he still needed money to get back to England. Sooner or later, he was going to have to steal some, just to stay alive.

Such considerations would be entirely irrelevant he told himself, taking tiny sips of his beer, if only Henri would show up at this bar like he was supposed to, and pay Jack the ten thousand euros he owed him. Not so long ago, Jack would have considered this a paltry amount, not even worth collecting in person, but now it seemed like a fortune.

That had been the arrangement. This bar. Place Saint Georges. Toulouse. At two o'clock. And if he failed to show on the first day, then he would almost certainly be there on the second, and if not then, definitely the third. He had whispered this down the phone to Jack from the bar in Marseilles where they had originally been due to meet, exactly one week previously.

"It's not safe here," he had said. "The cops are all over me. We'll meet in Toulouse. Nobody knows me there. I'll meet you there in a few days, and I'll have your money."

Jack had little option but to agree. He might not have trusted Henri, and he certainly wondered if this change of plan was really a ploy to avoid paying him, but there was no way he was going to pitch up in a bar that might be under surveillance by the French police, especially in Marseilles, where *les flics* had a justifiably fearsome reputation.

And so he was back in this bar again, waiting for ten thousand euros that was rightfully his, but which with each passing day seemed less and less likely to be coming his way.

Ten thousand euros would get him through the next couple of months, he thought to himself for the umpteenth time that day, and then it would get him back to England, at which point he could call in some favours to tide him over, and plan his next move. But if he didn't get the money, and right then that seemed a depressing certainty, he wouldn't be able to plan anything more than his next meal, his next bed and his next bus ticket.

Jack considered himself to be a tough character; resourceful, resilient, calm in a crisis, and not at all the sort of person who was prone to self-doubt or self-pity. Up until then he had always prided himself on being philosophical about the vagaries of life's twists and turns, with a long honed ability to accept his lot, and make the best of it.

Even on the day he had been taken to prison he had maintained an outward calmness of expression, thanks to this inner peace of mind, even if the nod of thanks to the judge as he was led from the dock had been more about bravado than respect for the judicial process that had just sentenced him to a ten-year prison term. His behaviour had been very much in contrast to that of his co-defendant, who had been dragged away screaming obscenities at anyone who would listen, and which Jack had been forced to endure from his adjacent cell beneath the courtroom, as the man wailed about the myriad injustices he had encountered in his life, and how they had led him to this sorry point.

But Jack never saw it like that. For him, it was all about risk versus reward. The Post Office in Tooting they had robbed at gunpoint had been worth the risk – they had stood to gain something in the region of two hundred thousand pounds if they had been successful – because the risk had been so small, and the reward so great. It was sheer bad luck that they had walked out of there just as an armed police unit drove past, returning to base after a false alarm in another part of the city, and sheer good luck when they had not been shot dead, when Jack's rather dim accomplice had waved a gun in their direction. Dim accomplices had been the blight of Jack's career.

So from Jack's perspective, a few years in prison – only five, as it turned out, after time off for good behaviour – was an unavoidable hazard of his chosen occupation. Sooner or later, you were going to go to prison, he told himself that day, and on the long days that followed. Be grateful that it wasn't sooner, and it's not going to be for longer. You don't have to be happy about it, but you do have to accept it, because the alternative is to drive yourself insane fretting about it.

And so Jack tended to be philosophical about the ups and downs of life. It was one of his few real strengths. That, and his ability to adapt to circumstances.

Although Jack considered himself to be anything but cosmopolitan, he had left England on his release from prison, and he hadn't been back since. Whilst inside he had struck up a friendship with a British drug dealer from Malaga, who had fallen foul of a recent extradition treaty, and was doing three years for conspiracy to supply narcotics, which he cheerfully admitted was far less a sentence than it might have been if the prosecution had made a better fist of its case.

His name was Bob Stern and he was a great enthusiast for his adopted country.

"Are you going straight back there, when you get out?" Jack asked him one evening while they played what felt like their millionth game of pool in the recreation hall.

"The day I'm released I'm on the first plane out there," said Bob. "The law can't stop me because the wife and kids are naturalised Spanish, need their dad, etcetera. If they didn't let me back, they'd be infringing my human rights or something. You should come out when you finish your bit. You'd love it – sunshine, beaches, birds, booze, drugs, everything a man could want. Great for people like us. If you play it right, that is. Seriously, come over and see for yourself, and we'll go and hit the spots. Might even be some work in it for you. Something better than knocking off post offices."

"It's a date," said Jack, not really thinking that he would ever go there. At that stage in his life he had never even left the country. But the picture Bob painted for him almost every day, of this magical sunny land so far removed from Pentonville Prison, must have permeated somehow, and on his release, partly due to a lack of other options, Jack found himself drawn there. And so he had broken his parole, skipped the country, and begun what he had come to think of as the foreign phase of his life.

Bob let him stay in an apartment he owned near the marina. There was obviously a price to be paid for this largesse, unspoken initially, but nevertheless understood, and as Jack had both hoped and anticipated, he became a small cog in the ex-pat criminal underworld of southern Spain, which he found had a good deal more compensations than its south London counterpart. And within a short time, because he was bright, and he could hold his nerve in a tight spot, and because he didn't overindulge in the product, he became an ever larger cog in Bob Stern's operation.

He had a couple of good years helping Bob run dope across the water from Morocco, and then everything changed when his benefactor crossed the wrong person in Tangiers whilst negotiating a deal, and ended up face down in an alleyway with a fatal gunshot wound to the back of the head.

"Bloody shame," one of his associates said to Jack at the surprisingly well attended funeral in Malaga a few days later. "Bob wasn't really into violence; he was too much of a gentleman for his own good and thought everyone else would be the same. Very trusting. Probably why he ended up in that alley. Where we'll all end up eventually."

Jack didn't want to end up dead in an alley, but he didn't want to give up the life, either. Besides which, he saw opportunities for himself in Bob's demise.

He stayed in Malaga, and tried to pick up where his late employer had left off, but with him running things and doing it his way. He'd hoped that his personal closeness to Bob and his family would enable him to enjoy a level of access in Morocco denied to some of the more senior members of Bob's crew, and that his bolder and more ambitious approach to business would yield greater dividends.

But it didn't work out like that. Bob Stern had got where he had by assiduously building a network of contacts over many years. He had done the hard yards, put in the time, spent the hours in sweaty cafés, sipping tea and smoking cigarettes, always being respectful, making the right personal connections, and establishing a reputation for being someone who was serious, and who could be trusted. He'd paid his dues. Jack, on the other hand, was a nobody, who was only where he was because of Bob's patronage. It had rankled with Jack when Bob was alive. It put him out of work after he was dead.

So Jack moved on, and formed a new partnership with a dealer from Marseilles, with whom he had done a small amount of side business in the past without Bob knowing. His name was Henri, and right then he should have been meeting Jack in this bar.

Henri may have had all the right contacts in Morocco, but Jack soon realised that his operation in France was a shambles. His distribution network consisted of a rag-tag crew of Algerian street kids, overseen by Corsican middlemen and enforcers. Their security was so poor that the densest of *flics* could have penetrated it, as they evidently had, and there was equal pressure in the other direction, in the form of a rival gang threatening a turf war. Jack quickly decided he'd be better off out of this particular enterprise, and for the first time since leaving Pentonville he had a yearning to go back to the old country.

Added to which, there was a Russian problem, and if one's business is crime, then nobody wants a Russian problem.

Henri had been buying Ecstasy from a dealer in Genoa called Boris Kerensky who was part of a gang that operated out of Saint Petersberg, and who were now looking to broaden their operations into the hashish business. Jack's business.

Jack had met Kerensky, at Henri's insistence, in a café his associate had a stake in, situated in the drab outskirts of Marseilles.

"He works for the Russians," he had said to Jack on the way in. "Play nice. They're the future."

Kerensky made much of his connections back east right from the outset, and Jack took an instant dislike to him. He was a lank figured, pale faced man, with greasy blond hair, thin lips and cruel eyes. He dressed in black leather and wore a silver pentagram on a cord around his neck. He had a faint lisp to his voice, and a way of looking past you into the middle distance when he spoke to you. The backs of his hands, and his fingers, and for all Jack knew the rest of him as well, were covered in a multitude of intricate tattoos, an ink maze of bizarre pictograms and Cyrillic script. Jack knew enough about gangs to know that this was a Russian prison thing, and that it marked Kerensky out as an ex-convict with some heavy duty connections.

Kerensky made no secret of his being part of the Russian underworld, and seemed to take pleasure in the thought that Jack might find that knowledge uncomfortable. Russian crime gangs had a well deserved reputation for ruthlessness. Jack had come across them in Spain. He had no wish to do so in France. Particularly with someone who looked like they'd come straight to this meeting from a witches' coven. Because Jack knew that behind this exterior appearance, unsettling enough though that was, probably lurked an even more unpleasant reality.

So he could have cheerfully strangled his feeble minded French associate, when he made the following pronouncement.

"Jack's got lots of contacts in Malaga; all over that part of Spain. I told you – he was part of Bob Stern's crew. Jack could handle the whole of the Spanish side, getting the stuff ashore; he used to do that all the time. And I'll handle the Moroccan end, and I'll use my Corsican guys to deal with it from here. You provide some investment, and give us protection here in Marseilles from the other gangs. And the police, too," he added.

An uncomfortable silence followed.

"So, what do you think?" Henri said at last.

Kerensky shrugged non-comittally.

"Jack?" Henri tried instead.

"Henri, could we have a word?" Jack said.

They spoke out in the car park, with Kerensky watching them through the window of the café.

Jack got straight to the point.

"Henri, look, firstly, don't ever count me in on a business deal you haven't even told me about, or talk about what I used to do in Spain to someone I don't know. And secondly, this guy is bad news, and his people back home are going to be even worse news. I'll level with you, Henri. I've got some serious doubts about your operation as it is. This Russian thing is a step way too far."

Henri looked down at his feet. Traffic roared noisily past them on the busy road.

"I'm sorry, Jack," he said at last. "But I need this, man. I'm into these guys for some other stuff, not just the E's, stuff you don't know about, and I need to get in with them on this one. I need them to put up the front money for Morocco, so I can get that moving, and deal with the other problem I have with them. It's a mess, but there it is."

He said something in French that Jack didn't understand.

"I'm sorry you're in this situation, Henri," he said. "I really am. But I would strongly urge you to re-consider hooking up with these people."

"I have to do what I have to do," Henri said with a sad shrug. "So Jack, I need to know, and I need to know now – are you in or out?"

"I'm out," said Jack. "Sorry, man."

"I'm sorry too, Jack. Sorry for getting you into this."

"That's okay," said Jack, even though it wasn't, pitying the hang-dog expression in front of him, and wondering just what sort of a hold these people had over his friend. "What's done is done. Good luck."

Jack left Henri standing there; didn't go back into the café; didn't speak to Kerensky again.

And that should have been that. Except there was a complication. Henri owed Jack ten grand from an old thing dating back to when they had been running dope in Spain, but Jack hadn't pressed him for the money thus far, as a gesture of goodwill, and as an investment of sorts in the business venture he had been thinking of forming with the Frenchman. But Jack hadn't put anything away during the good times with Bob, and he'd wasted money trying to set up his own partnership with the Moroccans, and now that the whole Marseilles thing wasn't going to come off, he was effectively broke and needed that cash.

And Henri had agreed to pay it to him at a subsequent meeting – their last, as it turned out.

He had been in an upbeat mood that day, compared to the Kerensky meet, and had hinted to Jack that the gang from Saint Petersberg was on board with his scheme, the deal had been struck, and the good times were about to roll again. He had hardly blinked when Jack mentioned the money he owed him. It was fine, he'd assured him, everything was cool. In his head, Jack could tell, he was already spending the fortune he was going to make with the Russians. What was a mere ten thousand? Things seemed settled, and Jack even found himself half-wondering if he had been right to walk away so swiftly from the Kerensky deal.

And then the police had chosen that precise moment to take a closer than normal interest in Henri's affairs, and the meet in Marseilles had to be called off, and the one in Toulouse arranged in its place.

Which was where he was now, back in this bar yet again, waiting for a measly ten thousand euros that he knew in his heart of hearts was unlikely ever to materialise, but which he felt he had no choice but to wait around for anyway.

Feeling depressed beyond measure, he broke his one beer rule and ordered another one. Another four euros, another one euro tip, because the waitress was hot and Jack may have been down on his luck, but he wasn't cheap, he told himself, as he counted down his wealth yet again. Eighty euros. Plus the three hundred at the hotel.

The old man was there again, he noticed. He had occupied the same corner table every day that Jack had been coming here. He was there when Jack came in, and he was still there when Jack left. He was always alone, never talked to anyone, and drank what looked like still water, all the time bearing a blank expression that seemed to convey a complete lack of interest in his surroundings.

He looked to be in his late sixties or early seventies and had silvery grey hair over a lightly tanned face, the only distinguishing feature of which was a set of unusually large eyebrows. He wore an expensive looking dark pinstripe suit, and there was a camelhair coat folded neatly on the empty chair next to him.

There was something oddly unsettling about his presence in the bar, Jack thought as he took a long draught of his second beer, and about his complete lack of interaction with the world around him. He wondered if he was slightly mad; if he sat there all day, sipping water and staring into space.

He turned back to the bar, his mind returning immediately to his predicament.

Why wouldn't the guy just show up and pay him what he owed him, he thought. Then he could be shot of this place and find somewhere to hole up for a few weeks, maybe down on the coast. It was early spring and the weather was getting warmer. He could kick back for a while, sit in the sun, and evaluate his options, rather than head straight back to London with his tail between his legs.

Jack suddenly became aware of a presence, like a shadow passing across him, and looked around to see the old man standing there. It was the first time Jack had seen him anywhere other than the table in the corner.

Maybe this will change my luck, Jack thought as he looked back down at the glass that was now two thirds empty. Maybe my useless partner in crime will finally show his face.

"He's not coming," said a voice beside him.

It was the old man, and he had spoken in English.

"Sorry, what?" said Jack.

"Your friend from Marseilles. He's not coming."

It was all Jack could do not to bolt from the bar as a myriad of scrambled thoughts poured into his head. What the hell was this? Was this a set-up? Was this guy with the police, or worse, from the rival drugs gang Henri had been knocking heads with, back in Marseilles? Was this how it was all going to come to an end, here in this bar in Toulouse, in the middle of a spring afternoon? Was the old man going to make some signal that would see agents spring up from the tables in the bar and pin Jack to the ground? Or would he be marched more subtly from here with a concealed weapon pressed into his side, and taken into an alleyway to be dispatched, just as Bob had been? Was this going to be Jack's Tangiers moment?

Making a huge effort to remain calm, he told himself to play for time.

"Sorry, mate. I don't know what you're talking about. I'm just having a beer. You must have me mixed up with someone else."

The man smiled.

"We both know that's not the case Mr Mears, but I took you unawares, so I'll forgive you for the lie you just told. It is, after all, a natural reaction to lie when suddenly confronted with an unpleasant truth, so I will not hold this against you, although I would most assuredly advise you not to lie to me a second time. So I repeat – your friend is not coming."

His voice was rich, mellifluous, the words enunciated in a tone suggestive of an expensive education. Normally, this would have been enough in itself to intimidate Jack, who was prone to a certain chippiness about his own origins, but on this occasion he had more pressing matters to concern him.

He knows my name, Jack thought. How the hell does he know my name?

"Who are you?" he asked the man.

"Let's just say I'm someone who happens to be in the right place at the right time. For you, that is. But you can call me Mr Smith."

"Mr Smith?" Jack said, unable to suppress a smile, in spite of the obvious gravity, as well as the downright weirdness of the situation.

"Yes. My name amuses you?"

"Not really. It sounds like a name you just made up."

"I did just make it up. It's not very original, is it? Except, of course, Smith is an exceedingly common name, so it's hardly an impossibility that it could be mine. After all, there must be a great many people in the world who have that name. Am I to assume that you would doubt their bona fides too if they presented themselves to you thus? And yet you sensed in my case that it was an invention. You are an intuitive person, I can tell. Would you care for another drink?"

"No, thank you."

"As you wish, but we may be here for some time, and it would be a shame if you had to dip into your meagre funds in order to buy your own drink."

"Look, mate," Jack said firmly, trying hard to assert himself. "I don't know who you are, and I don't know what your thing is, but I'm not going to be here with you for any length of time at all, because I'm leaving now, and there's not a thing you can do about it."

He felt better for saying this, and he felt his confidence return, but it soon evaporated when the man spoke again, this time with his voice lowered to a menacing whisper.

"Actually, there is a great deal that I could do to prevent you from leaving, but I have no wish to disturb these pleasant people around us. So, rather than me physically stop you, which I assure you I am quite capable of doing, let me just say this.

"Your friend from Marseilles is not coming. Not today. Not tomorrow. You are never going to see the ten thousand euros he owes you, and you have virtually no other funds. You wonder how I know this? Well, I just do. Deal with it."

Jack could hardly breathe. It was as if everything else in the bar had suddenly stopped and it was just him and the man in there. For the first time in his life he felt truly frightened. Who the hell was this guy, and how did he know so much?

"I know, I know," said the man, a kindness of tone returning to his voice. "You seem to be in a quite dreadful predicament. Of course, it is a predicament mostly of your own making, but your options are nevertheless terribly limited. You have no money and you have no prospect of earning any, added to which you are wanted by the police in four countries, including your own."

Four, thought Jack. Where the hell is the fourth one?

The man seemed to read his mind.

"Somebody talked in Tangiers," he said. "So, I ask you again; would you care for another drink?"

"Sure, why not," Jack said in a resigned tone.

The man motioned to the waitress that Jack had fancied in another age, and then glanced over at Jack's glass before putting a five euro note on the bar counter.

"Shall we?" he said, motioning over to the table where he had been sitting.

"What should I call you?" said Jack as they sat down.

"I told you," said the man. "Mr Smith."

Jack thought over his next move while the waitress brought his beer to the table. Try to take the initiative, he told himself.

"Okay, Mr Smith, I have a question. Who are you, why are you here, and how come you know so much about me?"

"That's three questions. Choose one."

"Why are you here?"

"I'm here to offer you something, Mr Mears."
"Offer me something."
"Yes."
"And what is that, exactly?"
"I'm here to offer you a once in a lifetime opportunity."
"Is that right?"
"Yes, it is."
Smith smiled and took a sip of his drink, while Jack gulped down about half of his beer, his mind furiously ticking over as he tried to work out what was going on. The scene was almost surreal, an effect accentuated by the Zen-like calmness of the man opposite him.
Play for time, he told himself again. Keep him talking.
"Are you here for the people in Marseilles?" he asked.
"No," said the man with a flicker of a smile. "I am never anywhere for anyone. Only for myself. But I do have some news from Marseilles that you should be aware of. About your associate in that city, the one you have been coming here and waiting for these past four days. I'm sorry to have to tell you this, but he's dead. Hence his non-appearance."
Jack gasped audibly at this news.
"I know, it's terrible," said the man, without a trace of sincerity in his voice.
"Did you kill him?" Jack asked.
"No. But I know beyond doubt that he's dead. Would you like me to tell you how he died?"
No, I really wouldn't, Jack thought.
"Okay," he said. "How did he die?"
"He was shot."
"Oh, really?"
"Well, initially. I would guess that his being shot was more of a disabling measure. He was shot in the stomach, which is a most painful place to receive such a wound, and this itself would have been enough to end his life

eventually, but in this case it was merely a precursor to what was to follow."

"What was to follow?"

"Yes. He was badly tortured. He was burnt with cigarettes, some bones were broken, and one of his eyes was removed. I dare say that the recently inflicted gunshot wound to his stomach also presented certain opportunities to his torturers."

"Did he talk?"

"I would imagine. Wouldn't you? But if he did, it was not enough to save his life."

"So how did they actually kill him?"

"He was crucified."

"What?"

"In a manner of speaking."

"In a manner of speaking? What does that mean?"

"It means he was nailed to a door through his hands and feet, and then left to bleed to death" said the man in a matter of fact tone.

Jack felt as if he might faint.

"I've never heard of that happening before," was all he could think to say, as he imagined himself being pinned to a door, with long nails ripping through his flesh.

"It's practiced in certain circles," said the man. "It's by no means commonplace. You could say that your associate was particularly unlucky to meet such an end. Even more so to be the recipient of some rather gruesome finishing touches."

"Finishing touches?"

"There's really no delicate way to put this, I'm afraid. You see, after they nailed him to the door, his assailants sliced off his genitals and stuffed them into his mouth. Barbaric in the extreme, and unnecessarily dramatic as well, don't you think? Whether or not he was alive by this stage I really couldn't say, but I would hope for his sake that he wasn't. Anyway, at some point during these macabre proceedings, he bled to death."

The man picked an olive from a small dish and inspected it carefully before putting it into his mouth. Jack noticed that he had beautifully manicured hands, with fingers that were long and slender, like a woman's.

"So," he said finally, after what seemed like an age. "To re-cap. Your friend is not coming, because he is dead; you will not be getting the ten thousand euros you are owed; and your own funds are diminished to the point of non-existence. And you are in a country where you no longer have friends or associates to call upon.

"In addition to this predicament, you are being sought by the law enforcement authorities of France, Spain and Morocco, as well as those of your own country. I would imagine it's only a matter of time before at least two of those nations' police forces pool their resources in this matter, such is the communitaire spirit of the age, thereby making you a potential case study in the successful workings of Interpol. And of course, as a convicted felon, there will be no shortage of archived material for your pursuers to base their search upon. Your photograph, fingerprints, modus operandi – all well known to those who need to know.

"If only that were the least of your worries," he finished with a sigh.

"What do you mean by that?" said Jack, defeated now, and no longer doubting the word of the stranger, despite the complete inexplicability of the whole situation. In that moment he realised that he was almost reconciled to his fate, whatever that might be, and then he thought of his erstwhile colleague, choking to death on his cock and balls, and he felt his chest constrict, and a flush of sweat run down his back.

"There are others pursuing you," said the man who called himself Smith. "Prominent among them are the associates of your late friend, who hold you responsible for this death."

"But I'm not responsible," Jack said pathetically, sounding as desperate as he felt, and showing more weakness to this one old man than he ever had to anyone else in his entire life.

"That is unfortunate, I agree" said the man. "People get confused, at times of great crisis, and rather tend to clutch at straws, you being one such straw, I presume. But there it is. Anyway, you should understand that what the street life of Marseilles have in mind for you pales into insignificance compared to the fate in store for you, should you have the misfortune to fall into the hands of those who butchered your friend, and who are, as we speak, looking for you.

"They're Russian," he added. "Need I say more."

"No," said Jack in a whisper as he contemplated this latest development, feeling suicidal for the first time in his life.

Russians, he thought. Boris Kerensky's people. He'd suspected as much as soon as he heard of Henri's demise. Jack thought back to their meeting, and pictured the man with tattoos on his fingers at the scene of the crime, as poor Henri bled to death in humiliated agony. Whatever it was that Henri had been into with that man, he had paid a terrible price for it. And somehow Jack was implicated. Guilt by association. One stupid meeting in a café that Jack hadn't wanted to go to in the first place, and that he had ducked out of almost as soon as it started. But as far as the Russians were concerned, he and Henri were partners, and thanks to whatever wrong end of the stick Kerensky had picked up that day in the café, and thanks to whatever bullshit Henri had fed him beforehand, not to mention whatever had got blurted out while having his dick chopped off, Jack had made enemies of people he didn't even know.

Jack stopped feeling sorry for Henri.

Because this really was the worst situation of his life. Jack was what in everyday parlance would be termed a hardened criminal, and pretty hard with it, but there were certain things one just didn't get into, and the Russian underworld was definitely one of them. He'd always taken great pains to avoid having any dealings with them in the past, for it was a well known fact that these guys played for keeps, and there were no lengths that they would not go to in order to defend their interests, their turf, their honour. He'd heard some hair raising stories, before Smith's grim little anecdote, about the things they would do to their victims, like putting their private parts in vices, and even pushing red hot irons through their chests. Now he had crucifixion to factor into the mix; something else to dwell upon in the fearful pre-dawn hours. Jack would have preferred to go back to prison than fall into the hands of such people. Not that prison would offer any sanctuary from them, he reflected.

The man's voice jerked him from this unpleasant reverie and back into the café, and his immediate predicament. As in, who the hell was this guy, how did he know so much about Jack, was he indeed Russian mafia himself, and was this whole surreal scene the prelude to his getting whacked the moment he stepped out onto the pavement?

"Come again?" said Jack.

"Forgive me, I should have guessed that you would be feeling a little distracted at having been brought up to date with developments. I was merely saying that you appear to be in a quite desperate situation."

"Listen mate," said Jack, "If you're here to do me in then just get on with it. You seem to hold all the cards. So why don't we just go outside and get it done? I really can't be bothered any more."

"Oh, the defeatism in that statement; the self-pity. This is not at all the Jack Mears I've come to know."

"And how exactly do you know me?"

Jack almost spat the words.

"That's more like it," said the man, looking him straight in the eye. "I'm glad to see there's still a little backbone in there. For a moment I thought I might have misjudged you."

"Whatever," Jack said wearily.

"Oh dear, and now such petulance from someone who has just been offered a most fortuitous lifeline."

"Do you want to run that by me again, while we're at it?" said Jack, feeling better for this little flash of defiance. "That whole once in a lifetime opportunity part? I wasn't exactly clear on that."

"Momentarily," said Smith. "But before I do, and in order to forestall any further questions on your part as to who I might be, how it is that I know so much about you, all the various whys and wherefores of this matter, let me offer a word of counsel.

"There are things in life that one needs to know, and there are things that one doesn't need to know. And there are also things that one would be better off not knowing, if only for one's peace of mind. But know this. I am who I am. Who I say I am is irrelevant. That I am who I am is all that matters. And you are who you are. And here's the rub. I seem to know all about you, and yet you know nothing about me. But actually, that's of little importance. And that's what we need to understand if we're going to get past this impasse and proceed to business. Because know this also. I have the power of life and death over you. I know that must sound like a bold statement from someone who has only just made your acquaintance, but there it is. Stark, but true. An unalterable fact. It's one of the things you need to know. And you can question that incessantly, if you choose, but it gets you nowhere. Because the answers to those questions are things that you don't need to know. So my advice to you would be simple.

"Go with it. In a nutshell, that is my counsel. Go with it, Mr Mears. Accept this situation that you have found yourself in, and use it to your advantage. Because to do otherwise will lead only to the kind of unpleasant end recently suffered by your friend."

He paused to take a sip of water.

"Forgive the peroration," he said. "I thought it best to clarify matters. Have I made myself clear?"

As he said this he set down his glass with great exactitude upon a coaster, and fixed Jack with an intense stare.

And in that moment, Jack realised that he was going to do what the man asked of him, and not just because of a distinct lack of options. He was going to do it because he was now as entranced by this person as he was intimidated by him. He felt like he'd been hypnotised. For some reason, he just knew that this path that had suddenly opened before him was one he was going to take, wherever it might lead, and however bizarre the circumstances of it's being offered. So he decided to accept his fate. He was going to go with it.

"Yes, you've made yourself clear," he said.

"I'm glad," said the man, with a hint of a smile.

Jack felt an easing of the atmosphere, as if the tension and antagonism had gone out of the room. He wondered about asking the man for another beer.

"So," he said. "What's this offer?"

"Like I said, a once in a lifetime opportunity."

"Tell me more."

"I have a job for you."

Here we go, thought Jack.

"What kind of job?" he said.

"A very simple one, as it happens. One day's work. Tomorrow. Finish by midnight. Payment, one hundred thousand euros."

Jack absorbed this with mixed feelings, whilst trying to keep his expression neutral. A hundred grand would be the best payday he had ever had by far, and would more than alleviate his present difficulties. But that kind of cash probably meant it was a hit job he was about to be pitched. Aside from whacking someone, you only made one-off money like that by either selling something, and Jack didn't have anything to sell, or stealing something, a task he didn't have the time to set up, given the imminence of the project. But calling in a hit was something you could do at short notice, if you had to, provided you had the mark's location, and the opportunity was there, and you could get someone to do it for you; someone desperate, say, and with no prior connection either to the person contracting out the work, or to the target. Someone just like Jack, in other words.

Jack was convinced that he was going to be asked to kill someone, and that made him uneasy. It was less of a scruples thing, and more of a having the bottle for it sort of thing.

"You won't be required to kill anyone," said Smith, seemingly reading his mind again.

"What will I be required to do?" said Jack, feeling relieved.

"Drive me to the frontier."

"Come again?"

"Well, Mr Mears, to put it in its most simple terms, I'm asking you to give me a lift."

"For a hundred grand."

"Yes."

"Sounds a little steep. Why don't you hire a limo?"

"Because I'd rather be driven by you," said Smith. "It's really quite straightforward. At around lunchtime tomorrow you will go to a garage just behind the railway station and collect a car that is waiting there. You will be expected. You will then pick me up from my hotel at exactly two o'clock and we shall drive out of the city, heading south and then west in the direction of the Pyrenees, with you depositing me at my destination some time later that evening, probably at a little before midnight."

"For a hundred grand," Jack repeated.

"Yes, but that part's non-negotiable," said Smith.

"Huh?"

"Sorry. That was an attempt at humour on my part. I am very well aware that I'm offering you a princely sum of money for what appears a simple, even banal task. That, of course, is the beauty of it, from your perspective. I would imagine it'll be the easiest money you ever make. So let's just say that if I were in your predicament, this is a gift horse I wouldn't be walking away from. However, if you insist upon looking in its mouth, as it were, and if you feel my offer is too generous, then I'm happy to expand your duties for the day. Would you like to serve as my bodyguard as well as my driver?"

"Are you in need of protection?"

"Not in the slightest. I'm merely trying to make your employment more fulfilling for you."

He gave the thinnest of smiles as he said this. Another attempt at humour, Jack presumed.

"Besides," Smith went on, "I do have a few stops to make along the way. You can hold my coat and briefcase, if you wish. Would that make you feel less as if you were taking advantage of the absurd generosity of an eccentric old man?"

Jack shook his head. This was crazy, he thought. This made even less sense than Smith knowing all about him and his affairs. There had to be a catch somewhere.

"A whole afternoon and evening sounds like a long time to get to the Spanish border," Jack said, changing tack. "We could get to the Pyrenees from here in a couple of hours."

"Scenic route."

"I see."

"And as I said, I have some errands to run."

Jack gave a sigh and sank back into his chair.

"It just doesn't make any sense," he said. "You must see that."

"You only say that because you're fixated on the sum of money involved. It's a large sum, to one such as you, and so you see the offer of this amount, for what appears so trivial a task, as being in some way inappropriate. But for me, the sum itself is trivial, its value insignificant. So our perspectives are completely different."

You really like the sound of your own voice, don't you? Jack thought, but didn't say. Well, okay then. I'll take your money if you really want to give it to me so badly. I'll be your superannuated chauffeur for the day. And if this is all an elaborate ruse so that I end up face down in some mountain ravine, then so be it, because it's where I'm headed anyway. I might as well get paid for my troubles.

"I sense that you've come to a decision," said Jack's new employer.

"Yes, I have," said Jack. "I'll do it."

"Congratulations."

He took a plain white envelope from the breast pocket of his jacket and passed it to Jack.

"Here are the directions to my hotel, and to the garage where you are to collect the car. And a ten thousand euro advance on your fee."

Jack couldn't suppress a grin at this news.

"Yes, indeed," said Smith, "There's a certain irony in that, isn't there? You will walk away from here this afternoon with the ten thousand euros you came to collect, after all. How serendipitous. Do what I ask of you tomorrow, and I'll pay you the other ninety at the frontier."

As Jack made to pocket the envelope, the man put out an arm to restrain him.

"Don't do what I ask of you tomorrow," he said, "Or fail to make our rendezvous, and I'm sure I don't need to tell you that I will know exactly where to find you. When I do so, the rather distressing scene in Marseilles that I described to you earlier will seem like a giddy burlesque, compared to what I will have done to you."

Jack stopped spending the ten grand in his head, and felt a sickening lurch in his stomach. Smith's eyes, which for some reason appeared quite black, seemed to be boring into him. Jack felt small and frightened again.

"Forgive me," said Smith, his mood lightening as swiftly as it had darkened. "I'm sorry to have to end our conversation on such a sombre note, but I'm sure a professional like you understands the importance of spelling out the terms of a contract, before it's undertaken. So as to leave no room for confusion."

"I understand," said Jack. "I won't let you down. We have a deal."

"And I'm already looking forward to our drive in the countryside. Good. We're done here."

Jack felt as if he was being dismissed, and got to his feet.

"See you tomorrow," said the man called Smith.

"See you at two o'clock," said Jack, and with that he turned and walked out of the bar.

As soon as he stepped onto the pavement he wondered if he was about to get whacked after all, but he didn't feel the tell-tale tap on the shoulder, no car screeched to a halt in the street in front of him, and he realised that what had just gone before wasn't some kind of sick joke preamble to a contract killing. Which didn't mean such a thing wasn't on the cards, of course. But not then, and not there. Right then, that was enough for Jack.

A once in a lifetime opportunity, he said to himself.

He turned out of the square and into the maze of side streets that surrounded it, and was soon in one of the less salubrious parts of Toulouse. This was the sort of gritty working class neighbourhood that Jack had grown up in back in England. It was little more than an urban slum, and until a few days ago, when his financial situation had become truly parlous, he'd believed it to be the kind of place he'd left behind for good. Smith's money would help to insulate him from such an environment for a while longer, he thought to himself, and since Jack had never felt much in the way of solidarity with his fellow man, this led him to look more with distaste than pity at some of the poor wretches he passed in the street, poverty etched into their faces as they made their way to and from whatever dead-end job or dead-end life they happened to possess.

I will soon be leaving your miserable company, and living the good life once again, he thought. Provided I stay alive.

Although he had been walking in the general direction of his hotel he came to a stop, as he had known he probably would, outside a drab and anonymous building with graffiti daubed on the boards blocking up its windows, and the accumulated soot and filth of several decades clinging to its walls. The place looked abandoned and deserted, as it was supposed to. It was only the aluminium faced door with its heavy duty locks that gave any hint that there might be more to this building than met the eye.

Jack only knew about this place because his late associate from Marseilles had told him about it, and suggested it might be somewhere for Jack to spend some down time while he waited for the imminent arrival of the ten grand. A few nights ago, back when Jack was choosing to believe that the arrival of his money was indeed imminent, he had blown some of his dwindling resources in this building. Now he was in the mood to return, and sample some of his new found prosperity.

He rapped on the metal door and a few seconds later he heard the shutter being pulled back over the peep hole. This was followed by the sound of a lock turning and a bolt being pulled.

The door was opened by a heavy set man with a protruding gut and with bare, fleshy arms that were covered in a multitude of tattoos; a mishmash of amateurishly drawn shapes that Jack the ex-con recognised as jailhouse tats. The man's head was completely shaved, and he had unnaturally small and beady eyes over the sort of mashed up features that spoke of a lifetime of beatings. He gave Jack a quick once-over and then stepped aside to let him enter.

Jack passed through a dimly lit hallway and climbed the stairs to the first floor where a crudely drawn sign pointed him down a corridor, towards another metal door. The man from downstairs must have rung up to say he was coming because as Jack approached the door it buzzed and swung open.

He stepped into a corridor which quite belied the building's drab exterior and the drear utilitarianism of its vestibule. Here, the floors were plushly carpeted, and the walls were washed in a tawny light and decorated with the sort of erotic artwork that befitted one of the most celebrated bordellos in Toulouse.

Jack had visited better establishments than this, and he had visited worse, and he thought the reputation of this place was a little overrated, but in that moment, with a pocket full of cash for the first time in a long time, its existence felt particularly fortuitous.

The Madame emerged from one of the doorways, and flashed him a look of recognition. She was a voluptuous woman who wore a diaphanous dress that displayed her ample cleavage, and Jack felt a tightening in his crotch as she swayed over to him.

"Ah, English, you come back," she said. "I hope you bring more money with you this time."

She was referring to Jack's first and last visit to this place, a few nights previously, when he had been forced to make do with a scrawny little thing barely out of her teens, whose skills were as limited as the time he could afford to spend with her.

"Much more money," said Jack.

As he said this, he reflexively put his hand to his pocket and felt the reassuring bulge of the envelope he had been given by Smith.

"I am pleased," said the woman. "And it is a great pleasure to see you here again," she added, almost sounding sincere. "Would you like to see the same girl as last time?"

"No, I would not" said Jack. "I'd like to see someone much better, please, and I'd like to see her for a long time."

As he said this, he laid five crisp one hundred euro notes down on a table beside her.

The woman gave a little murmur of pleasure.

"Oh, yes, of course," she purred at him. "Go to the room at the end of the corridor, and I will send my best girl to you."

Jack took out the envelope again, and counted out another five hundred euros.

"I have a better idea," he said."Send your two best girls to me."

The woman smiled and her tongue flicked across her lips.

"As you wish, Monsieur," she said.

Jack was half-way down the corridor when the woman called out to him.

"So, English," she said. "Did you win the lottery or something?"

"No," said Jack, grinning at her. "Somebody just changed my life."

II

The Devil's Armchair

The car was a sleek black Jaguar with tinted windows and it looked brand new.

Well, I don't suppose Smith was going to get driven to Spain in any old piece of crap, Jack thought as he stood in the garage forecourt, waiting while the eager to please owner of the premises fussed around, showing him how to pop the trunk and the bonnet, and demonstrating the car's various gizmos and gadgets, whilst randomly pressing upon him the registration documents, a spare key and the code for the radio.

Smith obviously has some pull, Jack thought. This guy was hopping around like a cat on hot tiles, all the time speaking rapid French that Jack had no chance of understanding.

Meanwhile, Jack tried to look as unimpressed and insouciant about the whole thing as possible, as if picking up a shiny new Jag was something he was quite accustomed to, and not worth getting excited about on a warm and sunny spring afternoon. Certainly not worth getting as flustered as the guy handing over the keys, he thought.

But he was secretly delighted. He had always loved this make of car, had actually owned one for a while, back when he started to make a decent living in Spain. But his late associate had persuaded him to let it go, said it looked too ostentatious for a Brit like him to drive a car like that around a place like Malaga; it might draw unwanted attention, etcetera. So Jack had relented, resentfully, wondering what the point was in taking the risks, if one couldn't live the life, and by then more than a little fed up with his partner in crime's cautious approach to everything and his general aversion to risk taking.

And yet it was he who had ended up gunned down in an alleyway in Tangiers, Jack reflected. Funny the way things worked out. Just as it was funny that the first car he had ever stolen was a Jaguar, black like this one, more years ago than he cared to remember, somewhere in Merton Road, south London. He hadn't liked parting with that either, but it was the first decent money he had ever made from a piece of work; his first proper pay packet. Happy days.

In fact, Jack was feeling quite cheerful himself, just then, in keeping with the sunny weather. He had stayed at the bordello until late in the evening when, finally sated, he made his way back to his unspeakable hotel, gathered up his few possessions, took a taxi over to one of the city's swankier establishments, and booked himself into the most expensive suite on offer, paying cash to a bemused night clerk. After sleeping soundly for the remainder of the night he got up, bathed, ate a gargantuan breakfast in the hotel dining room, and then went out and spent some more of the advance he had gotten from Smith on new clothes and toiletries, before returning to the hotel to check out and make his way over to the garage.

It had felt good to spend money again. It had brought back his confidence. Jack had decided to set aside his considerable misgivings about Smith and let events take their course. What would be, would be, he told himself. If Smith had wanted him dead then he probably would be by now, and whilst Jack had little doubt there would be a twist in the tale at some point during the day's activities, he had decided that he could live with that. Besides, he thought, anything was better than hanging around in a bar, day after day, waiting for ten grand that wasn't going to come.

So he was going to roll with it. For the time being. Until he needed to do otherwise. He was happy to see how things panned out. Really felt okay with that. Had decided to, anyway.

The garage owner finally completed his unintelligible peroration on the wonders of the car and handed him the keys. There was a bead of sweat on the man's upper lip, Jack noticed, and he had a glassy look in his eyes, like he was in shock. He had detected a slight tremble in his hands too, when taking the keys. Truth be told, the guy looked terrified about something.

Weird, Jack said to himself.

He tossed a small tote bag containing everything he owned in the world onto the front passenger seat, and got into the car.

Just as he was about to pull away the man stooped down and rapped on the window. Jack pushed a button on the armrest and the window came hissing gently down. The sound of the street drifted in.

The man appeared to have regained his composure somewhat. He didn't seem quite so agitated, and he took a deep breath before addressing Jack, doing so for the first time in English.

"The petrol tank – it is full," he said.

"Okay, thanks," said Jack.

A long pause. It felt as if the man wanted to tell him something, but couldn't quite find the words.

"Good luck," the man said, finally. "May God protect you, Monsieur."

Jack waited another beat before saying anything, trying to read the guy but failing to do so.

"Good luck to you too," was all he could think to say.

The man gave an odd little shrug, and then stepped back so Jack could drive off.

"Correction, very weird," Jack said to himself, aloud this time, as he pulled away. The last thing he saw in his rear-view mirror before he turned the corner was the man standing stock still in front of his garage, watching him drive away.

Jack eased the car into one of Toulouse's busy thoroughfares and headed towards the hotel where he was to collect Smith. He had plenty of time to make the two o'clock rendezvous, and whilst he would have liked nothing better than to have spent that time tooling around the city's fancier boulevards, enjoying the feel of the new car beneath him, and luxuriating in it soft leather seats, there was something he needed to do.

He pulled off the main drag and into a narrow side street, along which he drifted slowly, the car's engine barely audible, looking for somewhere to park up.

He eventually found a vacant spot in front of some kind of warehouse. He looked around and saw nothing to concern him. It was a down at heel sort of neighbourhood of shabby apartments, thrift shops and ethnic food places. On the other side of the street a woman of indeterminate age wearing shapeless clothes herded a group of young children along the pavement. Despair was engrained into her features, and she looked utterly worn down by life. She glanced over at Jack with a blank expression and then continued on her sorry way.

Jack got out of the car, took another quick look up and down the street and walked around to the trunk, which he opened.

It was empty inside. He leant in and ran his hands over the tautly carpeted surface. Delving into the corner he pulled back the carpet to reveal the spare wheel in its recess. He lifted the wheel out, saw nothing beneath, put it back, and smoothed down the carpet. Satisfied, he turned his attention to the car's interior.

He climbed in and lay down across the back seat, then felt beneath the two front ones. Jack's chief criminal activity was smuggling so he knew all about concealment. This was Smith's car, not his. There was no way he was going to drive off in it without checking it out first. For all he knew, it could have contained a body, now happily discounted, a cache of drugs, which was looking unlikely, although he'd have to strip it to be sure, or even a ticking bomb, which if it was anywhere would probably be attached to the chassis, or under the bonnet. Jack was saving that bit till last.

Jack finished patting down the car's floor, and then pushed his hands deep behind the back seat. He then moved round to the front and repeated the process, before checking the glove box, the ash tray and beneath the mats in each foot-well.

Not even a sweet wrapper.

Bracing himself for the bit he was dreading the most, he flipped the catch for the bonnet, got out and peered in.

Clean as a whistle.

Finally, he lowered himself to the ground to look underneath. As he did so two men walking past stopped to look at him, part enquiringly, part menacingly. Both were thick set and tough looking, and wore identical black leather jackets, making them appear like a couple of off-duty doormen from one of the seedy nightclubs nearby, which they may well have been, Jack reflected as he observed them from his crouched position, feeling not the slightest concern. He carried a certain amount of muscle too, and was more than capable of taking care of himself, and he was usually able to convey this to others. This occasion was no exception, and after staring the men out for a few seconds, they turned and walked away.

Lying on the pavement, Jack pulled a small pencil torch from the pocket of his jeans and scanned the underside of the car. It was almost as squeaky clean and shiny as everything else, and nothing appeared out of the ordinary.

His task completed, Jack got to his feet. The car was clean, as far as he could tell. One less thing to worry about.

He took his bag from the front seat and dropped it in the trunk, then got back into the car, turned the key in the ignition, felt the engine purr gently into life, and set off again.

He found Smith's predictably grand hotel easily enough, but he was still early, so he did a couple of blocks while he waited for the clock to tick over to the hour.

When he pulled up by the hotel entrance, Smith was stood waiting, looking straight ahead, motionless and expressionless. He was dressed the same as the day before. His camelhair coat was folded over his arm and he was carrying a slim black attaché case. He had no other luggage with him. He gave not the barest flicker of recognition or greeting as Jack approached, merely waited for the car to stop, whereupon he opened the rear door and deposited his case and coat, and then climbed into the front beside Jack.

"Two o'clock precisely," he said. "I like punctuality."

"I figured you would," Jack said as they drove away.

Jack headed for the main route out of the city on the southern side, and before long they left the centre behind them and started to pass through the mixture of suburbs, retail parks and light industrial facilities that formed a band dividing the heart of the city with the countryside beyond.

Smith said nothing during this period, merely stared with an expression of disinterest out of the window, and because Jack disliked uncomfortable silences he was keen to engage his passenger in conversation, and used the most obvious and easiest opening to kick things off.

"So," he said, "South, then, and after that west. I guess you want me to head for Carcassonne?"

"Not exactly," said Smith. "Or rather, not yet. I want you to bear left just up ahead where the road forks, and drive towards a town called Mazamet. From there we can take a route through the Black Mountains to our first stop."

"And where would that be, then?" said Jack, trying to sound breezy and carefree, although in reality these stops that Smith had referred to on the previous day were the cause of considerable concern to him. If there was to be trouble, this was where it was most likely to occur.

Smith said nothing for a long moment.

"You'll see," he said at last, before resuming his study of the passing countryside.

Worst possible answer, Jack thought.

"How about listening to the radio?" he suggested.

"I would prefer not to," said Smith.

Deciding that his companion was determined to be both morose and non-communicative, Jack resigned himself to a silent and anxious journey, and settled into his seat to try and enjoy as best he could the rare treat of driving a high performance car.

Everything about it felt smooth, well machined and luxurious, from the quiet rumble of the engine to the ostentatious softness of its leather upholstery. The dashboard, mounted in polished walnut, showed an array of lights, dials and digital displays that would have done justice to a small aircraft, and the steering wheel felt as if it was moulded to Jack's hands. As they emerged from the city onto the dual carriageway that went south, Jack gently pushed his foot on the pedal and enjoyed the feel of the car accelerating towards its top speed.

It was a pleasure to drive himself again, he realised, having travelled around France thus far on crowded buses and trains. He wouldn't have minded a little light conversation, though, or else some music on the radio. But it was Smith's charter, his party, and Jack was an employee for the day, so he could live with the silence.

They made good time and arrived in Mazamet less than an hour after leaving Smith's hotel. Smith did not speak at all during this period. In fact, he barely seemed to move a muscle, and merely stared out of the window.

But as they drove through the town he finally spoke, his voice sounding unnaturally loud after the long silence that had preceded it.

"Take this road," he said, pointing to his right. "Towards Carcassonne."

"Is that where we're going?" Jack asked.

"No," Smith said curtly, but then, as they started to climb out of the town and into the thickly forested slopes that surrounded it, he seemed to mellow for some reason, and shifted in his seat to face Jack.

"Do you like mountainous country, Mr Mears?" he asked.

"I've not seen that much," said Jack. "I've been to the Rif Mountains, in Morocco, for business, and a few years ago, when I was living in Malaga, I took a girl to the Sierra Nevadas, near Granada. We went to Ronda once too, which isn't mountainous, exactly, but it's quite rocky."

"Yes, I know it," said Smith. "I know all of those places."

"You've travelled a lot?"

"All over the world."

Jack curled the car around a huge sweeping bend in the road and saw that they were now high above the town. He decided to use the apparent thawing in Smith's mood to probe a little further.

"Where are you from, if you don't mind me asking? I mean, you sound English, but …" He let the sentence hang.

"I have a Swiss passport," came the reply.

"So, you're Swiss, then?"

"No, I have a Swiss passport."

"So, you're not Swiss?"

"No, I'm not Swiss. I'm not anything."

"Citizen of the world, right?"

"Something like that."

Another silence followed.

"Straight on, up here?" Jack asked, as a way of breaking it.

"Yes, indeed, straight on," said Smith. "This road goes right through the mountains, and eventually drops down to Carcassonne. But we will be turning off before then. I'll let you know when."

"Where are we going?" asked Jack.

"To an antiquarian bookshop."

It seemed an unlikely answer, given their surroundings, but Jack decided to go with it. He'd been doing that a lot in the past twenty-four hours, he reflected. It was his new philosophy. Until midnight, anyway. Assuming he lived that long.

With that sobering thought suddenly crowding his mind, Jack slowed the car behind a camper van that was crawling up the steep road through the forest. If he had been by himself he would have accelerated past it, but he sensed that Smith might not appreciate so risky a manoeuvre on a twisty mountain road. He decided to try shooting the breeze a little more.

"What brings you to France?" he asked.

Smith said nothing for a long moment, and Jack wondered if he was going to ignore the question, but eventually he spoke.

"I have come to France to attend to various matters of business," he said. "To meet with some associates and tie up a few loose ends. I am here, for the most part, for matters of little consequence; a mere fleeting visit."

Well, that tells me absolutely nothing, Jack thought.

He peered around the camper van and saw an empty stretch of straight road ahead. He pressed down on the accelerator and swept past the slow moving obstruction, casting a glance as he did so at his companion, out of concern that he might disapprove, but he needn't have worried. Smith seemed to have gone back into a trance, and was staring blankly ahead.

He's an odd one, thought Jack, not for the first time.

They continued on through the forest, seeing barely another car, just mile after mile of tree cover that was so dense in places that one couldn't see further in than the first row of pines, beyond which all was obscured by dark shadow. It made Jack feel hemmed in, as if he were driving through a steep canyon, impenetrable on either side. It felt claustrophobic.

"So where are these black mountains, then?" he said at last, in an attempt to jerk Smith from his reverie.

"We're in them," he replied. "If you wanted to see them, you'd have to be a lot further away. We shall be turning off in a moment. In a few miles you'll see a turning to the right. Take it."

Sure enough, a few minutes later, Jack saw the turn-off, slowed the car, and turned onto the road. As he did so, he felt the merest tremor of excitement blended with fear, as he anticipated arriving at their first destination.

If something's going to go down, he told himself, this is one of the places where it might happen. So get ready for anything.

Before long, they emerged from the forest into more open country; a scrubby terrain dotted with olive trees and outcrops of rock and bathed in late afternoon sunshine. In the far distance ahead of them Jack could see a range of hills running across the line of the horizon, and wondered where they were.

"The Agout Valley", said his companion, reading his mind. "We're going to a village there. It's called Montolieu."

"Is it far?" asked Jack.

"A few miles only. Along this road. When you get to the village, follow the road, and you'll come to a small car park off the main square."

"What's there?"

"Bookshops."

"Right."

A short time later Jack steered the car into the narrow streets of Montolieu. It was an unassuming sort of a place, pretty but not memorably so, with the usual assortment of church, Tabac and café with tables outside, and with some impressive views across the valley.

The village also contained a plethora of antiquarian bookstores.

"So I guess this is the place you go to in France if you want a second-hand book," Jack said as he manoeuvred the Jaguar into the tiny car park.

"One could say that," said Smith.

"Reminds me of Hay-on-Wye," Jack remarked. "A place in England," he added. "They have a lot of bookshops there."

"Yes, I've heard of it," said Smith. "Although I'm surprised you have."

"Forgive me," he said as Jack brought the car to a halt. "That was insensitive of me; assuming that someone such as you would be unaware of a place such as that. You may be a voracious reader, for all I know."

"No offence taken," said Jack, nevertheless gratified at this first sign of humility from his strange travelling companion. "I am quite a big reader, actually. Pretty much all there was to do in prison.

"But I wasn't in Hay to look for books. I robbed the post office there. One of the ones I got away with, before I got banged up. But I remember all the book stores from when we were casing the place."

They stepped out into the sunshine, and Smith retrieved his attaché case from the back of the car.

"I shall be no more than half an hour," he said. "Take a look around the village, if you wish, or there is a bar just over there. But please ensure that you are back here promptly. We still have much to get through today."

"You don't want me to come with you?" said Jack.

"No, that won't be necessary," said Smith, and with that he turned and set off down one of the narrow streets leading out of the square.

Pompous old git, Jack thought, as he watched him walk away.

He looked across at the bar and its smattering of drinkers sat outside enjoying the sunshine. Jack could have used a stiff drink himself, but he decided to stretch his legs instead and walk around the village, although he was careful not to follow the route taken by Smith.

Jack made his way along a narrow street, being sure to keep his bearings, so as not to get lost and miss the rendezvous back at the car. Smith's words from the day before, about the consequences of failing to fulfil his contract, weighed heavily on his mind.

This is the most bizarre day of my whole life, Jack thought, as he stepped into a small, sun-drenched plaza by a chuch. The peculiarity of his situation – the precariousness of it – crowded his mind like a persistent headache, and he felt depressed as he looked west towards the mountains; towards the place he was headed; the place where his fate would be made.

Sooner or later, somehow or other, this thing's going to play itself out, somewhere over there, he told himself. And to say he had a bad feeling about that would be the understatement of the century. He had the worst vibe of his life about it. But he felt so weirdly resigned to his predicament, it was like he was being marched to his own execution, and not bothering to do anything about it. It was a strange blend of fear and apathy.

He turned away from the vista across the valley, its prettiness doing nothing for him, and looked over at the church, and as he did so a pleasant looking woman walking two young children by the hand smiled a greeting at him as they went past.

Jack attempted a friendly mumble and then watched them walk away. The children wore uniforms and had satchels slung over their shoulders, and were presumably on their way home from school. For the first time since prison, he wished he lived a normal life; wished for once he was part of the world around him, and not existing on the fringes of it.

He stared at the silent edifice of the church.

Never found any inspiration there, he thought.

He started to make his way back into the heart of the village, walking along another narrow street, and one in which every other property seemed to be a bookshop. Jack slowed his pace to take it in and peer through some of the windows as he ambled by, imagining he was a normal tourist for a few moments. Jack liked to think that he possessed an aesthetic sensibility, for all his hard edges. He was bright, and had acquired a modicum of self-education. He liked nice things, and believed he had good taste, certainly in comparison with most of his compatriots in the criminal fraternity, and particularly compared to the new gangs from the east, whose vulgarity was as legendary as the violence and savagery they so routinely employed when attending to business.

In fact, Jack reflected to himself, this was just the sort of place he wouldn't have minded whiling away an hour or two in some imagined, idealised future; on one of those long dreamed of days after the one big score that would set him up forever; that mythical payday that everyone in the life believed was at least a distant possibility, despite all evidence to the contrary. But you had to have dreams, and Jack could imagine mooching about a place like this, everything nice and mellow. He liked books too, as it happened.

The various establishments looked as if they had stood there for many years, passing from one generation to another, their architecture becoming ever more weathered, and judging by some of the items on display in the windows, their content was similarly antiquarian.

The shops were small, hemmed in sort of places, with books from floor to ceiling; row upon row of cracked leather. They appeared cool and dark inside, in contrast to the heat and brightness of the street; like little dens of tranquillity. Most of the shops had window displays; glass shelves laden with rare and expensive looking volumes, some of which stood open to reveal the pages within, together with maps and prints and journals.

Jack stopped and stared at one such frontage, which strongly suggested an occult theme within. A pentagram had been painted onto the shop's fascia and a black silken backdrop to the window display was adorned with the same symbol. A painting hung across the top of the assemblage, depicting a hellish scene – a gathering of wretched looking souls in some blasted and rock strewn landscape, cowering at the feet of a demonic figure wearing a goat's head mask.

Just what you wouldn't want to wake up to in the morning, Jack thought as he scanned the titles of the books on display, noticing words like *daemon*, *necromance* and *magick* embossed onto the leather spines.

He looked at a book that was propped open on a small lectern. One of its pages was covered in a dense and miniscule script in some unknown language, but it was the facing page that drew Jack's attention. It was an illustration of a man being hung upside down from a gibbet in the grounds of a castle, while a hooded figure stood beside him, wielding a lash. Next to him stood a woman, also hooded, but with the cloak beneath pulled open, exposing her breasts. She was holding a club by her side, the head of which was covered in spikes. There was a fire burning, and its flames were licking close to the head of the man being hung upside down. A child crouched by the fire, staring at the condemned man. Looking more closely at the child, Jack noticed a tail protruding from the short cloak it was wearing.

Jake stared intently at the bizarre and horrible drawing before noticing something else. Beyond the book on its stand, in the shop's gloomy interior, Smith was standing with his back to him. A rotund man with a goatee beard was beside him, holding a book open with one hand, while with the other he was turning its pages, and seemingly pointing things out to Smith, who looked like he was nodding in recognition at something.

Jack watched as the man flicked through the book, and then it occurred to him that it might not be the wisest course of action to spy on his new employer, and so he backed warily away from the window and continued on down the street.

As he went past the shop's door he noticed it had a Fermé (Closed) sign on it. Smith must have been a valued customer, Jack reflected. A valued customer at some loony tunes black magic store. Nothing to worry about there, then, he thought wryly to himself as he walked away, wishing that he still smoked.

Jack made his way back to the car and considered driving off without Smith, but of course he immediately thought better of it.

It was late afternoon by then, and the sun was starting to drop down towards the line of hills on the other side of the valley. Jack couldn't help but feel a sense of foreboding as he anticipated the coming of the night; as he imagined being alone with Smith in the darkness on some deserted mountain road.

Smith arrived back at the car shortly afterwards. He sauntered into the little car park carrying a book under his arm and greeted Jack with something approximating a cheery smile.

"I hope you enjoyed your walk around the village," he said as he got into the car, having returned the attaché case to the back seat, but having kept hold of the book, which he was now opening across his lap.

Jack wondered if this sudden flush of bonhomie from Smith was the result of his recent acquisition, and presumed this was the book he had seen him looking at in the shop.

Maybe he'll lighten up a bit now, Jack thought.

They drove out of the village and for the next little while Smith guided Jack along a series of minor roads until they reached a highway running parallel to the high ground to the west, which they turned onto, heading south towards Carcassonne. He did this distractedly, barely looking up from his book, as if from memory.

The countryside was more open here, Jack noticed as they sped along the straight road; more fertile, too, being covered for the most part in swathes of vines showing the first signs of leaf. Small farmsteads lined the road every few fields or so, and tractors moved in clouds of dust along the horizon.

Smith closed the book he had been so engrossed in, the snap of it closing sounding loud above the soft thrum of the engine, and making Jack start slightly.

"A short distance ahead, you will see a sign for a vineyard, off to the right," he said. "That's where we're going next."

"Right," said Jack. "What's there, then?"

"A vineyard," Smith said.

"I know. I meant, what's the purpose of our visit? If you don't mind me asking."

The older man paused before replying.

"No, I don't mind you asking," he said finally. "We're making a social call, nothing more; visiting some acquaintances of mine."

"Right. Social call."

"Yes. And this time you may accompany me, Mr Mears. There will be no need to stand outside and press your nose to the window."

Jack gulped slightly.

"Yeah, sorry. I was just walking around, having a look at some of the books in the windows."

Guy's got eyes in the back of his bloody head, he thought.

"There's no need to apologise," said Smith. "It's a small village. Our running into one another was not exactly beyond the realms of possibility. Did you see anything that interested you? I'm sorry that our visit was so brief, and you didn't have time to have a proper look around. That book in the window seemed to get your attention. What was it about it that interested you, may I ask?"

"Oh, nothing really," said Jack. "It was just because it was open, I suppose. I thought the picture in it was quite interesting. It was of a man …"

"… Being hung upside down, while being flogged," Smith finished for him.

Jack felt a shiver go down his spine.

"You know it, then?" he said.

Smith said nothing for a long moment, and Jack started to feel uneasy.

"No, I never saw it before today," he said at last. "I looked at it in the window as I left."

He gave a low chuckle.

"Forgive me, Mr Mears, I was toying with you. But I was keen to see what had aroused your curiosity, hence my pausing to look for myself. Did you like what you saw?"

"I don't know if it's a case of liking it or not liking it," said Jack. "I was just taking it in, really. I wouldn't have been able to understand the text, anyway. It was probably in French."

"Actually, it's in Latin."

"Well, there you go."

"Indeed, but one could be forgiven for not understanding Latin; it's very little taught these days. But I would have thought that a knowledge of French – the language of the country you are in, after all, and in which you are trying to outwit the authorities, and certain adversaries – would have been quite useful. You might consider learning, if you plan to stay here. You have some rudimentary command of Spanish, I presume, from your time in that country."

"Yes, a bit of Spanish," said Jack. "Not much French, though. Do you speak French?"

"Yes. And Spanish. And Latin. The turning's just here."

Jack saw a turn-off ahead, marked by a wooden sign mounted on a post, and from which a rough track led off the road and up a steep, vine covered escarpment.

He slowed down, and turned from the smooth tarmac of the road onto the roughly made up track, feeling the change in texture through the wheels of the car. As he turned off, he glanced up at the sign but the script on it had weathered almost to nothing, save for a single word that Jack didn't have time to read.

"So, how many languages do you speak, then?" he asked Smith as he drove slowly up the track through the corridor of vines, getting ever higher above the floor of the valley.

"All of them," said Smith.

"Really? Sorry, that sounds hard to believe. You're exaggerating, I take it?"

"Perhaps so, perhaps not. You would seem to be in a singularly poor position to judge. But forget the text in that book for a moment. Recall what you thought of the picture that faced the text. It was an arresting image, was it not?"

"Yes. Not one that I'll forget easily."

"I would imagine not. Did it remind you of anything?"

"Should it have done?"

"I wondered if it brought to mind the ritualistic demise of a certain former colleague of yours, in Marseilles."

Not until now, thought Jack.

"Is there a connection?" he asked warily.

"Only in the broadest generic sense; not in any of the specifics. So there's no connection at all, really. But I wondered if it might have made you think of it."

"I'm trying not to think of it," said Jack.

"Most wise."

By now they had reached the top of the escarpment, and the ground had levelled out to reveal more fields of vines that stretched all the way to the edge of a range of high hills, down which the last rays of the afternoon sun were pouring, casting a warm glow onto the plateau they now found themselves on. The route was clear ahead apart from a small wood in the middle distance.

"Stop here," said Smith as they drove up to the dense copse, into which the track disappeared, to re-emerge, presumably, on the other side.

Jack stopped the car as instructed. He could make out the dim outline of a house within the gloomy thicket. For some reason he felt a strong urge to stay out in the sunny openness of the fields, rather than venture into the dark wood, but he forced himself to follow Smith, who was already walking purposefully away from the car, carrying his book.

As they entered the wood and got closer to the house, Jack's sense of foreboding grew. It was a stone building, quite substantial in size, suggesting a large family home, and there were outbuildings off to one side, and a pair of garages, outside which was parked a pickup truck. But it was anything but homely. The shutters on the windows were all closed, the garden was overgrown, and the place had a neglected, dilapidated feel about it. The only sign of life was a trickle of smoke coming from the chimney.

Smith led Jack down a poorly defined path strewn with weeds and clumps of long grass, and up to the door of the house. He knocked loudly – three sharp raps – and a moment later it was opened by one of the most peculiar looking people Jack had ever seen.

The man was old, at least eighty, with long white hair framing a weather beaten face with wizened features. He had a hooked nose from which tusks of hair were sprouting, and eyes that were such a dark shade of brown that they appeared almost black. When he smiled a greeting, the gold in his teeth seemed to glint at Jack from the gloom of the house's interior. He sported two large, hooped rings in each ear and a spider web tattoo covered one part of his forehead. He was dressed in a dirty looking black suit over a dirtier white shirt that was open at the neck, revealing several gold chains, and he wore a black trilby hat pushed back at a jaunty angle that had a feather in its band. When he raised his hand to beckon them in, Jack noticed that he had a ring on each finger.

He and Smith appeared to be well acquainted, and as Jack followed them into the house they chatted away to each other in familiar terms in a language he couldn't understand, although it didn't sound like French.

They passed through a dimly lit hallway into a large kitchen that was only marginally less dark. A woman and a young boy stood almost as if to attention with their backs to a large range, as if Smith were a distinguished visitor, and upon entering he went straight over to them and greeted the woman by taking her hand and bringing it lightly to his lips. She nodded her head reverentially in response. He then put a hand on the boy's shoulder and said something in a soft tone that Jack couldn't hear.

Smith then turned to face the room and spoke some more of the odd, guttural sounding language as he pointed at Jack, eliciting nods from the others.

"I just introduced you, Mr Mears," he said. "These are some dear friends of mine. I shan't waste your time or theirs with long introductions, since we won't be here for long. Suffice to say, the gentleman standing beside me is Mr Balthazar, and this is his family. Why don't you sit down for a few moments. Our hostess will serve you some tea. I have a small matter of business to discuss."

As he said this, the strange looking old man called Balthazar tipped his hat at Jack, and said something in a raspy voice to Smith, who cocked his head attentively.

"My friend says you are welcome to his home," he said. "Well, something like that," he added with a shrug.

The woman ushered Jack over to a chair in the corner of the room, and then turned her attention to a large pot brewing on the stove, while Smith opened his book on the kitchen table. Balthazar sat down to inspect it while Smith remained standing, looking over his shoulder. The boy hadn't moved a muscle since they came in, and merely stared at Jack.

The room was infused with a chill, pervading murk, the only illumination being whatever light could squeeze through a small, grime encrusted window, and the flames of two black candles, burning on a sideboard. There was a cloying, rotten smell in the air, as if there was something dead in the room.

Resisting the urge to run outside into the light, and feeling more spooked than ever by this strange little household in this insalubrious place, Jack lowered himself nervously into the chair he had been offered. Smith was now pointing at something in the book, and the two men were talking excitedly to each other, their voices taking on an almost sing-song tone, and at one stage Jack could have sworn he heard the old man make a whinnying sound like a horse.

He looked over at the woman, who had her back to him as she busied herself with the tea. In many ways, her appearance was as odd and striking as that of the man of the house.

She was about Jack's age, somewhere in her middle to late thirties, and she might have been attractive, but she was so heavily made up it was difficult to tell. She was garishly dressed for the countryside, Jack thought, and would have stood out in town, too. She had on a short red dress that was barely a slip, and that was pulled tightly across her ample breasts and posterior. The black fishnet stockings she wore had a ladder in them that stretched all the way up the back of her thigh, before disappearing into the red folds of her dress. She had a small, mohair cardigan that was little more than a wrap draped across her shoulders, and wore high heeled shoes that clacked on the tiled floor when she moved.

She seemed to sense Jack looking at her and turned to face him. She pouted suggestively with lips that were smeared with … Jesus, was that black lipstick, Jack thought? She was a bizarre sight in the middle of the woods, that was for sure. There was something brazenly lascivious about her that reminded Jack of the two whores from the previous night.

Not that Jack felt in any way aroused. There was a deathly aura about the scene; something other-worldly, like a bad dream, that was making him feel a real sense of dread inside.

And nothing was causing him to feel more unnerved at that moment than the young child who continued to stand stock still on the other side of the room, staring at Jack with blank, expressionless eyes.

He couldn't have been more than ten years old, but he gave the impression of being older, perhaps because of the grown-up clothes he was wearing – a black suit like the old man at the table, who was presumably father or grandfather to him – and the stillness of his posture, which implied the discipline of an older child. Although ostensibly smart in appearance, Jack noticed stains on the collar of his shirt, and dirt caking his hands, and his hair looked greasy and unkempt. His face was the most ghastly white pallor, and he had dark hollows around his dead, glassy eyes. Not the slightest glimmer of life came from him. It was almost as if he wasn't there; as if he was a ghost.

The woman came over carrying a cup of steaming liquid. She stooped slightly to pass it to him, and then remained that way for longer than she needed to, allowing Jack a view of her cleavage. She had a musty smell about her, making him think of old leaves.

He thanked her as he took the cup, and she swayed her hips provocatively as she walked away.

He peered suspiciously at the contents of the cup. It looked like tea of some kind, and smelt aromatic and faintly pungent. He blew away the steam and took a tiny sip and was pleasantly relieved when it tasted of nothing more exotic than herbal tea. He took another sip and watched the two men at the table.

The old man with the long white hair appeared engrossed in the book as he slowly ran a pointed fingernail across one of its pages, whispering softly to himself, while Smith looked on approvingly. They appeared almost as master and pupil. Smith pointed something out to the man, who stared wide eyed at the page for a moment, and then let out a loud, guffawing laugh that sounded more like the braying of an animal than anything human.

There was something feral about these people, Jack thought, as if they had been out of contact with the world for too long, hidden away in this dark wood. Even though it was but a stone's throw from the highway, Jack felt as if he had entered another world, and it was one he was feeling increasingly eager to leave.

Not wanting to just sit around any longer, he put down the tea and stood up, nodding with his eyes over at Smith as he did so.

"Toilet?" he said enquiringly.

Smith said something to the old man, who looked at Jack and pointed out to the hall where they'd come in, and then said something unintelligible.

"Down the hallway, second door on the left," said Smith.

"Merci," Jack said to the old man, who flashed a mouthful of gold in response.

Feeling relieved to be out of the room, Jack made his way down the dark hall, passed one door that was closed, then came to another that was slightly ajar. He pushed it open and flicked the light, to find himself in an utterly nondescript cloakroom. He wasn't quite sure what he'd been expecting but he felt the tension of the situation ease slightly. He did, however, detect a faint trembling in his hands while he was peeing.

This house had really got to him, he thought. He didn't normally get spooked like this. He didn't believe in the supernatural, and he thought occult establishments of the kind he had stood outside that afternoon catered to people who were mostly sad, weird and soft in the head. Not that he'd have said so to Smith. But this place had got under his skin, and awoken some long suppressed, primordial fear in him.

He went back into the hallway but he didn't feel like returning to the kitchen, so he hung back for a moment. The house felt cool and damp around him, as if it wasn't lived in. Jack wondered if the people in the kitchen were squatters. Cobwebs hung from the ceiling and every surface seemed to be covered in a fine layer of dust, so much so that Jack felt like he was breathing it in.

A staircase of dark timber swept upwards into the gloom, and Jack wondered if there was anyone else in the house, but he wasn't inclined to go up there and find out. Instead he went further down the hallway, knowing that if he was caught snooping there, he could at least make out that he'd been looking for the way back from the toilet.

There was another door at the end of the long passageway that drew Jack's attention. The door was shut, as the one next to the toilet had been, but this one had been secured by a hasp and padlock. Jack walked over to it, moving as quietly as possible, conscious of the hum of voices coming from the kitchen.

The padlock was a large one and looked brand new, very much in contrast to everything else in the house. Jack wondered what could be locked behind that door that was of such value.

As he turned to go back he heard a muffled sound from within the room. Then he heard it again – a metallic sound, clearer now. Pressing his ear to the wood, he strained to hear. It sounded like a chain being dragged across a stone floor. Jack's mind spun. Could there be a person locked in that room? Someone chained up?

Against all his better instincts, he knocked softly on the door.

Silence.

Jack knocked again, slightly louder this time.

He heard a different noise; a human noise. It sounded like someone crying. A man crying, Jack thought, but it was hard to tell. What the hell was going on here?

And then Jack froze, as the hairs went up on the back of his neck, and he knew instinctively that someone was behind him.

Not wanting to turn around, but knowing that he had to, he slowly turned from the door, tensing his body.

He found himself face to face with Smith, staring at him with dark, pitiless eyes.

"Impressive sixth sense," he said, after what seemed like an eternity.

"Come on, we're leaving," he said, turning smartly on his heel.

Jack followed him back into the kitchen, where he made a show of finishing his tea and smiling his appreciation, while Smith said farewell to the strange trio, crouching to whisper something to the boy, who was still standing in the exact same spot, and whose eyes had locked onto Jack as soon as he had re-entered the room. Jack felt heartily glad to be leaving. As they walked out of the room Jack noticed that Smith had left his macabre book on the table, but he didn't feel minded to tell him. Perhaps it had been a gift for the old man, he thought.

When they got outside it was as if a weight had been lifted from his shoulders. The sun felt warm on his face, and the sound of birdsong was welcome in his ears. It felt like he could breathe again. Walking away from the house, Jack couldn't resist sneaking a glance back, as if he needed to check that they weren't being followed, but there was no-one there, and the house looked as dead inside as it had when they approached it.

As they made their way back to the car, Jack wondered about the locked room, and whether it did contain someone being held in chains who had cried out to him, but he decided that it was none of his business, and whatever it was, he was well out of it.

Jack noticed Smith watching him as they walked.

"You seem a little unnerved, Mr Mears," he said.

"Just glad to be out in the fresh air," Jack said.

"The appearance of my friends alarmed you, perhaps?"

"They seemed a little unconventional," said Jack.

"Oh, they are most certainly that, and much more besides. But they are also kind, loyal and dedicated people, highly learned, and possessing an array of most valuable talents."

"I'll take your word for it," said Jack, rolling his eyes slightly, something he instantly regretted, when it became clear that Smith had picked up on it.

"Indeed you will," said Smith, coming to a halt by the car. "These people are very dear friends of mine, and I would ask that you refer to them with respect, and not in the sort of sarcastic tone you just adopted."

Jack felt Smith's dark eyes bore into him over the roof of the car.

"Sorry, I didn't mean to sound rude," said Jack, backtracking swiftly. "I just meant …"

"Yes?" said Smith, raising his eyebrows. "Do tell me what you meant."

Jack took a deep breath.

"I just meant that they seemed the sort of people that might be hard to get to know, but I'm sure that, once one did get to know them, they're very nice people."

Smith said nothing and continued to look at Jack enquiringly, as if expecting more.

"So I'm very sorry that I didn't have a chance to get to know them better," Jack finished.

There. Satisfied now, he thought?

"Good answer," said Smith, all smiles again.

"Let's go," he said. "I want to get to our next stop while we still have the light."

Jack started the car, turned around and headed back across the vine covered plateau. He noticed that the sun was dipping towards the range of hills on the horizon. The heat had gone out of the day and shadows were starting to inch across the landscape.

Jack drove carefully down the steep slope that led to the road, wincing inwardly as the rough surface attacked the car's suspension. It seemed worse than it had when driving up, for some reason, and Jack almost came to a stop at one point as he slowly negotiated his way around a particularly sharp piece of rock sticking out of the ground.

"So much care and attention to give to a car that isn't yours," said Smith. "Most commendable, although I'm sure this vehicle is more robust than this tortuously slow journey back to the road would suggest."

"Sorry," said Jack. "It's not much further. It's just a nice car, that's all. I don't want to damage it. I've enjoyed driving it," he added.

"I'm glad," said Smith. "I selected it with you specifically in mind."

"Did you now," said Jack.

"But of course. Does it remind you of anything?"

Yes, it most certainly does, thought Jack. It reminds me of the first car I ever stole, because it's identical in every detail, but there is absolutely no way you could know that, so I don't even want to go there.

"No," Jack lied. "It doesn't remind me of anything."

"Really?" said Smith, sounding surprised. "I thought it might have done. Oh, well. My mistake."

They had reached the junction with the road. Keen to change the subject from Smith's uncanny and impossible to explain knowledge of Jack's past life, Jack nodded over at the wooden sign with its faded script and one added, painted on word that he couldn't understand.

L'Enfer.

"What does that mean?" he asked.

"It means hell," said Smith. "Somebody's idea of a joke, I would imagine. Turn right; same direction as before."

Okay, let's find another subject, Jack thought, not wishing to dwell upon why it was that the place they had just visited had been so named, as a joke or otherwise.

"So where are we headed now?" he asked.

"Carcassonne," said Smith. "But we don't need to go into the city. Bear right at the outskirts, and follow the signs towards Perpignan."

"Are we going to Perpignan?"

"No. We're going towards Perpignan. Through the Aude Valley. There's a village there where I need to make a stop."

"Another social call?"

"No. The thing we are going to see is quite inanimate."

"Fair enough," said Jack, and they lapsed into silence as they sped down the long, straight road.

A short time later Jack looked in the rear view mirror and saw a vehicle following close behind them. With a sense of profound unease he realised it was the pickup truck that had been parked by the house in the woods, and that there were three people sat in the front.

"I think we're being followed," he said with a slight catch to his voice, betraying his fear.

Smith shifted in his seat to look behind them.

"No, we're not," he said.

"Sorry to contradict you," said Jack, "But I'm pretty sure that's the truck from the house we just visited."

"It is the truck from the house we just visited," said Smith. "But they're not following us. They merely happen to be going in the same direction."

"Are they going to this village we're going to?"

"No. I've asked them to go somewhere else, and to meet us later on."

"We're meeting them later?" Jack said.

"Yes, indeed. You must be pleased. You just told me how you'd like to get to know them better. Now you're going to have the opportunity, and much sooner than you might have thought."

"Oh, I am pleased," said Jack. "Absolutely. Couldn't be more pleased."

"Glad to hear it," said Smith.

The rest of the journey passed without incident. The traffic got heavier as they approached Carcassonne and Jack lost sight of the truck for a while, but as soon as they got free of the congestion on the outskirts of the city and headed west into more open country, it appeared behind them once again.

Jack could see the Pyrenees ahead of them now in the form of a jagged line of snow capped rock on the horizon.

We're entering the end-game, he thought to himself, his pulse quickening. Get ready for anything.

A short time later they drove into the town of Limoux, which slowed their progress as they worked their way through the clog of early evening traffic, and then they emerged on the other side into empty countryside that suddenly seemed wilder and more rugged than that which had preceded it. Thickly wooded hills rose all around them, and the road twisted its way along the course of a river, past plunging ravines and steep defiles. The sun had now dropped behind the mountains towards which they were headed as dusk descended upon the landscape. The sky had a reddish tinge to it that made Jack think of blood.

As they entered a small town called Couiza, with the truck still clinging to their tail, Smith told Jack to look out for a turning off to the left at a set of traffic lights. They shortly drew up at the lights, and as they waited for them to change Jack glanced in the mirror and looked back at the truck. Its three occupants were sat across a bench seat in the front, the man driving, the child sat in the middle, looking as blank faced and impassive as he had back at the house. Jack could have sworn the woman blew a kiss at him. He felt relieved when he turned off to the left and the truck went straight on, although he knew it was only a temporary reprieve.

"In a short while," said Smith, "You'll come to a junction at the foot of a mountain. Take this turning, and the village we are going to is a mile or so further on."

The terrain here was even wilder and more dramatic than it had been on the valley road. Jagged rock set in red earth covered a landscape of steep escarpments. Up on a high ridge to the left Jack noticed the burnt out remains of a castle. They were approaching a large mountain that appeared quite black in the fading light.

"Do you know this area?" Jack asked.

"Oh, yes," said Smith with a sigh. "I know it very well. You could say it's like a second home to me."

He spoke the words softly, with evident fondness.

They reached the junction which was dominated by the dark mountain. On the other side of the road was a smaller peak topped with white rock, and from which a rugged escarpment formed the other side of a steep valley.

Jack took the turning and steered the Jaguar over a narrow bridge and into the valley and a short time later they arrived in a village by a river. Signs advertised thermal baths and there was a bustle of people on the pavements lining the narrow streets. It was a pretty sort of place, with an air of faded grandeur about it. Its streetscape was a mixture of imposing municipal type buildings, dressed with flower pots and planters, and small painted houses. It was a hemmed in sort of place, slung as it was beneath a wall of rock, but in a way that felt cosy and welcoming, and as they passed by a square fringed with shade trees in which people were sat at café tables, Jack wished that he could have been coming here in different circumstances.

"Drive straight through the village," said Smith. "There's a car park just the other side. Stop there."

Jack drove along the line of the dark escarpment, following the course of the river below him on the other side, and just beyond the last house in the village, as the landscape started to open out, they came to a small car park, which he turned into.

"Am I coming along?" he asked Smith as they got out of the car.

"If you wish," said Smith. "It's not far. Just a short hike up into the woods."

Jack hesitated. If Smith's intention was to have him whacked, then the woods above this village afforded exactly the right sort of discreet, out of the way location. But Smith was offering him the option of either going or waiting behind, whereas if he'd had something planned, he would surely have insisted that Jack go along. Jack decided that he preferred having Smith where he could see him, rather than let him go wandering off by himself. And he felt like stretching his legs and enjoying the end of the day. Could be my last one, he reminded himself.

"I'll come along," he said.

They crossed the road and Smith led the way up a stony track marked with a footpath sign. They were soon beneath the trees and the fading light meant that it was dark beneath the leafy canopy. Jack felt the first slight chill of evening in the air.

They followed the path up the escarpment. Jack soon started to feel the effects of this exertion, the higher they climbed, but he noticed that Smith was striding purposefully ahead, putting distance between himself and Jack.

Seems keen to get there, Jack thought.

A short time later they emerged into a clearing, and as Jack caught up with Smith it was clear that they had arrived at their destination.

Standing just off the path was what could best be described as a stone chair. A large, lichen covered boulder had been cut so as to form a seat with arms, making it appear as a giant throne placed upon the hillside. It was an incongruous sight, in the middle of the woods; like a prehistoric rest area on the route of a nature ramble.

"Quite something, isn't it?" said Smith, as Jack approached. "Of course, this area wasn't always so thickly wooded, so at one time the views from here would have been much more impressive. But still, a fine perch from which to contemplate one's affairs."

"How old is it?" said Jack. "I mean, when was it carved?"

"A very long time ago," said Smith, running a hand lightly down one of its sides. "It is popularly known as *le Fauteuil du Diable*, or the Devil's Armchair. But to me, it's just the armchair."

"Can I sit in it?" Jack said.

"You can. People do. This is quite a celebrated spot, in its own way. But I would prefer that you didn't, Mr Mears. Not this evening."

"Whatever," Jack said with a shrug. "So, are we walking on, going back, staying here? What are we doing?"

"I'm going to rest here for a short period," said Smith. "You may find this difficult to understand, Mr Mears, but this is a sacred place for me. I would like to spend some time here alone. Would you therefore kindly move out of the clearing and onto the path lower down, and wait there for me. And as you're here, you can do something useful."

"What do you want me to do?"

"It's unlikely that anyone will venture up here, this late in the day, but if they do, I'd be grateful if you would prevent them from entering the clearing until I'm done here."

"Okay," said Jack. "But it's a public path. How am I supposed to stop people coming up here."

"You're a resourceful fellow," said Smith. "I'm sure you'll think of something."

Jack decided to say nothing more. He'd cross that particular bridge in the unlikely event that he came to it, he thought. He nodded his assent to Smith and started to make his way back to the path.

Once he was out of the clearing he ducked under some trees and settled onto his haunches to wait. He figured he was probably a little closer to Smith than he would have liked, but he was keen to observe him, and witness whatever it was that he was about to do by the strange stone chair. He edged a little further under the trees, took a quick look down the path to ensure no-one was approaching, and then turned back to watch the clearing.

Jack was pretty clear in his mind by then what his employer for the day was all about. The occult bookshop, the people at the house in the woods and now this stone chair, the chair of the devil. Smith was presumably the practitioner of some form of occultism or devil worship.

Well, fine, thought Jack. Voodoo bullshit and mumbo jumbo to me, but whatever rocks your boat, etcetera. Jack couldn't care less what people believed, or even what they did, as long as they weren't doing it to him. But whatever Smith was into was a factor, as far as the rest of the day was concerned, and Jack wanted to know as much as he possibly could about this person, in order that he be best prepared for whatever lay ahead.

And so he watched surreptitiously from within the thicket of trees, not really sure what he was looking for, or expecting to happen.

At first, everything seemed innocuous enough. Smith walked slowly around the chair as if he was examining it, and then he very slowly lowered himself into it, and rested his arms on its sides.

For several minutes, nothing happened. Smith barely seemed to move a muscle and merely sat in the stone chair, staring into the trees. Jack started to get bored, and thought about moving off, further down the track, and finding a nicer place to sit and wait. Besides which, he noticed, it was getting cold up there, even though there was still some light left in the sky. Must be the fact that we're high up, he thought to himself. Or maybe it was the brisk wind that was now blowing through the clearing and down the path, and which was rustling the leaves in the trees, whereas the air had been quite still before.

Jack then noticed a perceptible shift in the atmosphere around him. It had suddenly become much darker, like the light had been drained out of there, even thought the last vestiges of the sun were still visible through the trees on the far side of the clearing. Everything seemed oddly off kilter, for some reason. Either that or Jack was running a fever.

Smith seemed oblivious to all of this, Jack noticed. He continued to sit motionless in the stone chair, staring straight ahead, almost as if he was in a trance.

And that was when he turned in the chair to look back at him, and when Jack realised, with a sense of dread unlike anything he had ever known, just what it was that he was dealing with here. Because in that moment, and it was only for the briefest of moments, Smith's face completely changed. What it changed to, Jack couldn't say, because immediately after the temporary transformation Jack instantly forgot what this face had looked like, as if he'd awoken from a dream he couldn't remember, but knew that he'd had. But he knew that what he had seen had been hideous and terrifying, and definitely not human. And in that moment of revelation, Jack suddenly realised that he was dealing with something far more dangerous than he could possibly have imagined; realised that he was dealing with something that was literally beyond the realms of the imagination.

Smith didn't worship the devil. Smith was the devil.

Jack leapt to his feet and started to run down the track as fast as he could. No longer caring about his commitment to Smith, or whatever the hell that thing up there was; all that mattered to him now was getting away from this place as quickly as possible.

As he approached the bottom of the path, he skidded over some loose shale and felt his feet go from under him, but rather than fall straight to the ground, he careered through a line of bushes and then found himself in mid-air before ending up sprawled, face down, on a hard tarmac surface.

The road, he realised, and just as he started to pull himself to his feet he heard a violent shriek of brakes. Jack closed his eyes tightly and waited for the worst.

It never came. He opened his eyes to find himself inches away from the bumper of a car. The car's horn sounded, and then a torrent of French invective poured from the window.

Jack crawled over to the side of the road and the car drove off, its driver flashing him an angry hand signal, as he stared up pathetically from the ground.

He looked back up the slope and his worst fears were realised. Through the trees, he could just make out the dim form of Smith, coming back down the path.

Jack clambered to his feet and dashed across the road to the car park. He was determined to get away; determined to put some distance between himself and Smith, while he still could.

He reached the car and yanked on the door handle. Locked. Fumbling in his pocket for the key, he looked anxiously behind him. Smith had not yet emerged from the wooded slope. He still had a bit of time.

He unlocked the car and got in, his hands shaking as he gripped the steering wheel with one hand, and jabbed the key at the ignition with the other.

"Going somewhere, Mr Mears?" said a voice.

Jack screamed as he saw Smith sitting beside him in the passenger seat. He threw his body back against the door, as if he could somehow squeeze himself out of the car.

Jack had never felt more terrified in his life. His whole body was shaking violently, and he felt the blood drain from his face.

"What are you?" he stammered.

"Surely you've guessed by now," came the reply.

"You're the devil," said Jack, hardly believing he was saying it.

"Think of me as that, if you wish, although it's a highly pejorative term. But yes, for the sake of simplicity, I am what would popularly be thought of as the devil, though that is not what I am actually called."

"What are you actually called?"

"I really can't say."

"Why not?"

"Because there is no word in any human language for what I am. So my name is something that cannot be expressed in this world."

“This world?”

“As opposed to my world.”

“Your world? Do you mean hell?”

The demon smiled and shook his head.

“Please, Mr Mears, spare me the fire and brimstone sermon. There is no such place as hell; it simply doesn’t exist, any more than heaven does. Don’t believe what you read in the bible.”

“I’ve never read the bible.”

“A wise choice.”

“So that’s how you know all the languages,” Jack said under his breath.

“I beg your pardon?”

“Nothing. It’s just … I can’t believe this is happening. I don’t know what’s going on.”

He felt like he was going to cry.

“Nothing’s going on, Mr Mears. You’re giving me a lift. Nothing has changed, so do please try and get a grip on the situation.”

Jack closed his eyes and bunched his hands into fists to stop them from shaking, desperately trying to remain calm.

“So what is your world?” he said at last. “What is this place you come from?” In spite of the absurdity of the situation, or perhaps because of it, he felt himself relax slightly. It helped, somehow, to talk in these terms, and Smith’s conversational tone suggested that he was not going to be punished for running away.

“My world,” Smith said slowly, “Is a very beautiful and sacred place. It is a world strikingly similar to this one in its physical appearance, and yet it is completely different. It exists parallel to this one, you might say, and yet is quite removed from it.”

“What do you mean?” said Jack. “Where is it?”

“I’m sorry,” Smith said. “We really don’t have time for a lecture in metaphysics. Another time, perhaps.”

Silence hung in the air for a long moment.

"So you're very powerful?" Jack said at last.

"Yes," said Smith.

"And you can see things? I mean, that's how you knew all about me, my situation, what happened in Marseilles … all of that."

"Yes, indeed. I've been watching you, in a manner of speaking."

"Watching me," Jack repeated.

"Yes. Does that disturb you?"

"Yes … but actually I feel better for that. Because at least I know now. I know how you knew those things. I couldn't work it out before."

"I'm glad to be able to set your mind at rest."

"I wouldn't go that far."

"I suppose not."

"And if you can see me, then I can't really get away from you, can I?"

"No, you can't."

Jack took a deep breath before speaking again.

"And you're … sorry, I don't know how to phrase this … you're evil?"

Smith smiled and shook his head.

"That word has no meaning to me," he said. "I just am."

He spoke softly, calmly, looking not at Jack, but straight ahead, towards the river beneath the car park.

"And this just is," he went on, turning to face Jack. "So I trust this little episode, your flight from the forest, as it were, was merely an aberration, not to be repeated, and we may now continue our journey."

"What's going to happen to me?" said Jack.

"What's going to happen to you when?" said Smith.

"Tonight, later on, when we get to the frontier? What's going to happen to me? What are you going to do?"

"Nothing at all."

"Nothing?"

"No. You're going to drive me to the frontier, and I'm going to pay you a very large sum of money."

"And that's it?"

"More or less."

"More or less?"

"Yes."

"Right. Guess we should get going, then."

"I would appreciate it. After all, that is what I'm paying you for."

"Okay," said Jack as he started the car, scarcely able to believe what was happening.

"One more thing before we go," said Smith, his voice all business again, in contrast to the soft ruminations of the past few minutes. "When I said I intend to do you no harm this evening, I spoke the truth. However, let me make something absolutely clear. Do as I tell you for the remainder of the evening, and you will not be harmed, and you will be paid at the frontier, as I have promised. But pull another stunt like the one you just attempted in the forest, and I guarantee it'll be the last thing you ever do. Are we clear on that?"

"Yes," Jack said in a strangled voice.

"Good" said Smith.

"Shall we?" he continued, pointing out towards the road, his tone lightening again. "Come along, Mr Mears; let's have less of the mournful expression. We're nearly at the end. But we have a way still to travel, and much to do before we get there. Let's get to it."

Jack drove slowly out of the car park, feeling his hands tremble through the steering wheel.

"Left?" he said to Smith as they reached the exit.

"Left," said Smith. "Towards the mountains."

Jack pulled out onto the road, and with the light fading, he and the demon resumed their journey.

III

The Fallen

Jack finished the last of his food and drained his glass. He hadn't thought that he'd be able to eat, such was his state of shock and upset following the revelatory visit to the stone chair, and what had transpired in the car park afterwards. But somewhat to his surprise he had devoured a large bowl of stew and the best part of a loaf of bread, and had washed this down with two glasses of red wine. He must have been hungrier than he had realised, he thought, not having eaten since breakfast, and the food and wine even seemed to have calmed his nerves as well as filling his stomach.

Smith had not eaten. Presumably, Jack thought, demons did not require such sustenance, even when in human form. He had taken a drink though, a light port, whatever that was, but he had said little, so the meal had passed largely in silence.

They were the only customers in a small café-restaurant, in a village that sat on a hill beneath a ridge of high cliffs. It was a low key, rustic sort of place, and the food had been excellent. But now that the meal was finished, Jack was starting to wonder what was going to happen next.

They had driven away from the car park beneath the stone chair with the light fading fast, and with Jack in such a state of nervous anxiety that he had hardly been able to keep the car on the road. But as night had fallen, Jack had made a conscious effort to keep a hold on things, and he was now more determined than ever to get through the next few hours and claim his reward – his once in a lifetime opportunity – even if it was to come from such an unbelievably disturbing source.

They had followed the valley road for about an hour, seeing barely another car, and travelling through wild and desolate country. At one point they had driven around the base of a large mountain that Smith had said was called Bug-something, and was the largest peak in the Corbières - the rugged foothills to the Pyrenees through which they were now passing; the last stage of their journey before the great mountains themselves. They had driven through dark woods and rocky grasslands, containing only the odd hamlet or farmstead by way of civilisation. Eventually they had arrived at this village, on a hill topped by a windmill, and Smith had suggested they stop for a meal before proceeding to their next appointment, and although the last thing on Jack's mind had been food, he was in no position to argue otherwise. But now that he had eaten, he felt calmer, stronger and better equipped for whatever the night was to bring.

As Smith went to the counter to settle up, Jack took a deep breath and tried to gather himself as best he could.

It's just like before a job, he told himself. Like sitting in the back of a van, pulling a stocking mask over his face and checking his gun; or standing in the dunes on some deserted beach, waiting for a hashish run from across the water.

Or being about to get in a car with Satan and drive him to the frontier, he thought with a shudder. But it's just another job, right? Treat it like that and you'll get through it easier, and then you've got the rest of your life to wonder about just what the hell it was that went on tonight.

Smith said he meant him no harm, and why would a person, or being, with so much power bother to lie to someone as insignificant as Jack? If he'd wanted him dead he could have struck him down with a bolt of lightening, presumably, rather than go to all the trouble of undertaking a road trip to the Pyrenees, so why distrust his word?

Go with it. Maxim of the day.

"So, where to?" said Jack as they stepped out into the restaurant courtyard and made their way over to the car. It was a clear night and the sky was filled to the brim with stars, a tableau broken only by the dark, jagged rock of the escarpment that towered above them, while beneath them, the course of the valley was clearly visible, with the lines marking its patchwork of fields picked out by the glow of a full moon.

"Up there," said Smith, stopping to point up at the rocky ridge.

"Up there?" said Jack. "What's up there?"

"A person I wish to visit," said Smith.

"Right. Whereabouts?"

"Just there. See the light?"

Jack stared over at the mass of dark rock and saw the tiny, illuminated glow of a house, about three quarters of the way up.

They drove out of the village and followed the road up the escarpment. Dense swathes of fir trees were interspersed with outcrops of rock and high pastures, giving the scene a dramatic, alpine appearance, and making Jack feel strangely enervated, despite his anxieties. He realised that he no longer felt fearful, just on edge, even a little excited. This trip was feeling more and more like going out to do a piece of work, and during the short drive up the mountainside he decided that working for Smith maybe wasn't such a bad thing after all.

It proved to be a brief moment of respite. At Smith's direction they turned off the road and onto a stony track that led into the woods, and all went dark around them, and the temperature in the car seemed to drop perceptibly, and Jack remembered what Smith was, and he felt the confidence drain out of him.

He glanced over at his companion, who was half-turned in his seat to face him, and looking at him in an odd way. For a fraction of a second, his eyes seemed to glow yellow in the dark. Jack made himself look away. He was gripping the steering wheel so tightly it was making his hands ache.

They emerged from the woods and onto a large, grass covered plateau and Jack saw a house ahead, reminding him of the place where they had met Balthazar earlier, and he wondered if it was to be here where they would rendezvous with the strange old man and his companions. He looked around anxiously for the pickup truck and was thankful to see no sign of it.

Save that problem for later, he said to himself.

They drew up in front of the house. It was a battered sort of place that looked like it had seen better days. Light shone from the inside.

"Am I coming in with you?" Jack asked as he switched off the engine.

"No, thank you," said Smith. "This is something I must attend to alone. Feel free to get out of the car and stretch your legs, if you wish, but don't wander too far from this clearing. We need to be away from here promptly, if we are to remain on schedule."

Jack looked out at the thick mass of dark trees that surrounded them, and smiled to himself at the idea that he might be tempted to go ambling off into the forest in the dead of night.

Smith started to get out of the car and then turned to face Jack.

"One more thing, Mr Mears," he said. "When I said that I don't want you to follow me into this house, I meant it. Do not come in, for any reason whatsoever. Whatever you may hear, or think you may hear, don't even think about coming to investigate. Under any circumstances. Am I clear?"

"Of course," said Jack, barely able to raise his voice above a whisper.

"Thank you. Moments such as this are better dealt with alone and in private."

"Whatever you say," said Jack.

Jack watched Smith walk over to the house and up a short flight of steps to a dilapidated timber veranda. He knocked on the door; three sharp raps. A few moments later it opened, and the light of the house spilled outside. Smith stepped in and the door closed behind him, without Jack getting a chance to see who had been standing on the other side.

He sat in the car and listened to the silence; felt the thud of his heart. He wondered what was going on inside, and how long he'd be waiting here. Jack hated waiting, always had done, even though he had become conditioned to it in prison.

After a while, feeling restless and unable to sit still, Jack got out of the car. There was a strong breeze, this high up, and now that he was outside the insulated bubble of the car he could hear the roar of the wind in the fir trees. There was a hint of citrus in the air, and from somewhere in the woods Jack heard the sudden shriek of a bird.

He turned his back on the house to look down the mountain into the valley. He could see the lights of the village where he had just eaten supper far beneath him. He stood there and stared at the nightscape, forgetting for a moment about whatever was going on inside the house, and enjoying the beautiful starkness of the scene.

Maybe, when I get my money from Smith, he thought, I'll come somewhere like this and spend some downtime. He liked these sort of places; wild places; places as far removed as possible from the grim council estate in south London where he had grown up.

Money from the devil. How about that? Jack wondered if that was the same thing as making a pact with the devil, and decided that he didn't care. He wasn't religious; he had no stake in the fight; he only cared about what was coming to him; was completely at ease about that. Or he could rationalise it, anyway. Jack was good at that. One needed to be, if one was going to make a living out of crime, and happened to possess a modicum of intelligence. Jack had been rationalising his behaviour all his life, and this latest dilemma wasn't so very different.

Just as he was thinking this, a terrible scream pierced the night air behind him, and he spun around. The sound had come from the house. A second scream followed, even more anguished and protracted than the first, and Jack's heart started to race, as he wondered what to do.

Stay here, he told himself. Smith said to stay here, whatever happened. Whatever was going on inside that house wasn't his problem.

More screams followed; shorter, staccato shrieks that sounded part human, part animal. Jack had never heard anything like it. It sounded like someone was being tortured to death in there. Then the screaming stopped, and was replaced by the sound of something crashing to the floor, and glass breaking, as if a piece of furniture had been pushed over. This was followed by a long, blood curdling scream, and then there was silence from the house, and all Jack could hear was the wind in the trees.

A few moments later, Smith emerged from the house and walked towards the car, and Jack saw him throw something into some bushes, and then take a handkerchief from the breast pocket of his suit and wipe his hand on it.

"Ready, Mr Mears?" he called over to Jack.

At that precise moment, Jack had never felt less ready for anything in his life, and it took an effort of will even to approach Smith, given the violence he had just heard him administer. He wondered if he had killed the person in the house.

But Smith seemed as calm and impassive as ever, as if nothing untoward had just occurred.

"Beautiful night, isn't it?" he said as Jack walked over to him.

"I guess so. Is everything okay?"

"Of course. Why wouldn't it be?"

"No reason."

They got into the car.

"Sounded like there was a bit of aggro in there," Jack said as he started the engine, trying to sound as casual about the whole thing as possible.

"Yes, there was," said Smith. "A case of a recalcitrant employee who needed to be disciplined. Most unfortunate. It pained me greatly to have to administer such a punishment."

"What was the thing you threw into the bushes?" Jack asked.

"One of his eyes."

Jack felt his stomach lurch and he gave an audible gasp.

Calm down, he told himself. It's none of your business; it's not your problem. Just stay calm and get through this.

He noticed Smith watching him.

"If you're going to ask lots of questions, Mr Mears, then you have to accept that you're going to get some unpalatable answers."

"Yeah, right," said Jack, trying to sound relaxed. "Poor guy," he added.

"On the contrary," said Smith. "He is a very fortunate man indeed. I could have exacted a far more terrible punishment."

"Than removing an eye?"

"He has another one he can use. Luckily for him, I was in a charitable mood this evening. I can only hope that by extending to him the milk of human kindness, he will genuinely repent. We shall see."

Jack could think of nothing to add to this chilling little peroration and so he remained silent until they reached the road.

"So where to now?" he asked at the junction.

"Turn right," said Smith. "We need to go down into the next valley. Once you reach the main road, turn right again, and head in the direction of a town called Quillan."

Jack turned right as directed and they continued to climb the escarpment. As they reached the top, Jack imagined that the views from here must be spectacular in daylight. Even in the darkness he could see the jagged profile of a mountain range ahead of them, while below, the scattered lights of a few small settlements winked up from the blackness. It felt like being on top of the world.

They dropped down the steep road to the valley floor and entered a town. After negotiating some narrow streets Jack found the main road and headed in the direction of Quillan.

High ground now stood on either side of them, and Jack figured that the peaks to the left must be the Pyrenees.

We're getting closer, he thought. This is the end game. Starting now.

"Where are we going?" he asked.

"In about half-an-hour," said Smith, "You will see a turn-off to a castle on your left. Follow this turning, all the way to the castle. It's a popular tourist spot, so it will be well signposted."

He told him the name of the castle.

"We're going to a castle?" said Jack. "At this time of night?"

"Indeed we are."

"Won't it be closed?"

"I've made arrangements for it to be open."

Of course you have, thought Jack.

They didn't speak again. Smith seemed to sink into a trance, not even shifting in his seat, and after a while it was almost as if he wasn't there. Jack concentrated on the fast, sweeping road, and started to relax a little – or experience a degree of calmness, at any rate – as they barrelled through the night.

But when they eventually reached the turn-off to the castle, he felt his fear return like a great wave.

He drove slowly through a small village where there were no signs of life, and where not a single light shone from any building, and then out the other side into a wooded valley. A short distance later he saw a sign pointing to the castle and he turned onto a narrow road that led into the woods and then up a steep slope. Ahead of them now, he could make out the silhouette of a ruined fortress at the top of the thickly forested ridge. It made for a dramatic sight against the night sky.

"There's a car park just below the castle," said Smith.

They soon got to the car park, where Jack noticed another vehicle, parked in the shadows. As they got closer, he realised it was the pickup truck belonging to Balthazar.

Jack parked the car next to a wooden building that must have been the ticket office for the castle, but which was as dark and closed up as the village they had just passed through.

"The pathway to the castle is just there," said Smith, pointing over at the dark woods as they got out of the car. "It's only a short walk from here."

"What's up there?" said Jack.

"A most spectacular castle, now sadly ruined, and so not at all what it once was. I stayed here for a while, in the thirteenth century. You should have seen it then. It was a magnificent place.

"Interesting times," he added, almost as an afterthought.

Without even bothering to acknowledge this little anecdote that illustrated Smith's obvious immortality, Jack simply stated what was on his mind.

"What I meant was, why are we going there? What's going to happen to me up there?"

"To you? Nothing at all. Really, Mr Mears, you always seem to think that something is about to happen to you. It must be a very stressful way to live. I can assure you that you will be quite safe up there. I merely need your assistance with something. I assume that won't be too much trouble for you?"

"No trouble at all," Jack said tightly.

Jack followed Smith into the trees and then up a steep path strewn with rocks.

The castle walls appeared to their left and as they rounded a bend in the path Jack saw the entrance ahead of them. He thought he could hear the faint crackle of a fire coming from inside the castle enclosure.

It was a massive place, its huge walls rising above the line of the trees, looking thick and impregnable, in spite of their ruined state.

They crossed a narrow timber bridge and passed through the outer defences into the main body of what was left of the castle. As they did so, the sounds of a fire grew louder and Jack detected the murmur of voices.

Balthazar and his motley crew, he thought with a shudder, as he steeled himself for the encounter ahead.

But nothing could have prepared him for the scene he was about to witness.

The interior of the castle enclosure was encircled by high walls that appeared as a jagged line of rock against the inky black, star filled sky above, and Jack felt the wind on his face as he stepped through an archway and out into the large, grass covered courtyard. What he saw in its centre turned his heart to ice, and it was all he could do to restrain himself from running straight out of there, but of course Smith's presence beside him put paid to that idea as soon as it formed in his addled head. Instead, Jack stood there, aghast at what was in front of him.

A fire was burning within a ring of stones, and beside it stood three figures that Jack presumed to be Balthazar, with the woman and child. He could only presume this because they were all wearing cloaks, with hoods that obscured their faces, but there was no doubt it was them. The slight figure of the child was easily identified, as was the woman, who had opened the front of her cloak to expose her breasts. She was carrying a club by her side, the head of which looked to be covered in spikes or nails. The tall figure of Balthazar held a whip coiled in his hand. The child was holding something too, above his head, but Jack couldn't be sure what it was in the gloom of the night. It looked like a stick, and then he saw it move, and realised it was a snake.

But it was the figure hanging above the fire that really caught his attention. It was a man, alive but in evident distress, who had been stripped naked and hung upside down, his head inches from the flames, having been suspended from a crude looking timber gibbet. As if to emphasise his complete mastery over his captive, Balthazar marked Jack's arrival on the scene by uncoiling the whip he was holding and administering a savage lash to the hanging man's midriff. The sound ricocheted like a rifle shot around the valley, followed by a cry of anguish.

In a rare moment of clarity Jack realised that the man hanging above the flames must surely be the person behind the locked door in the house in the woods. That much, apparently, seemed clear.

But when Smith spoke it transpired that there was still something he was missing.

"Well?" Smith said expectantly, as Jack struggled to control the bile rising in his throat.

"Well, what?" he said back.

"What do you think?"

"What do I think of what?"

"You mean you don't recognise any of this?" Smith said, his voice conveying a tone of mild incredulity.

"Should I recognise it?" said Jack, now feeling bewildered as much as frightened.

"From this afternoon," said Smith. "From the bookshop in Montolieu. The book in the window. Surely you remember."

And then Jack did. The scene he was standing before was a replication of the one depicted in the book that had been open in the window of the occult bookshop. Smith, for some bizarre and inexplicable reason, had ordered that this scene be re-created for Jack's benefit.

"The book in the shop window," Jack said in a strangled voice. "It's the scene from the book in the shop window."

"The scene from *your* book," Smith said emphatically, signalling to Balthazar, who reached into his cloak and pulled a book from within its folds that he passed to his master.

"Your book," Smith said again, handing it to Jack.

"My book?" Jack said.

"Yes, your book," said Smith. "I'm giving it to you. You seemed quite captivated by this image when I noticed you looking at it through the window and so I decided to buy it for you. It's a gift. A mark of my appreciation for having so kindly been of assistance to me today."

"Thank you," Jack said, taking the book and wishing he'd never seen it before.

"I'm only sorry I couldn't give it to you earlier," Smith continued, "But it was necessary that I gave it first to Mr Balthazar, in order that he could put together this little assemblage for us, and I have to say, he has done a most splendid job, has he not?"

"Yes," said Jack, struggling to maintain his composure. "A really great job. It looks just like the scene in the book."

What else was he supposed to say, he wondered.

"I'm glad you approve," said Smith. "Now, if you don't mind, put down that book and step a little closer to the fire."

"Why?" said Jack, nervously.

"Just do it," Smith said sharply.

With great reluctance, Jack laid the book down on a pile of stones and edged closer to the fire. The poor wretch hanging above it was straining to keep his head above the heat of the flames. Jack saw that his body was covered in bruises, and it looked as if he had been beaten severely before being hung upside down from the gibbet.

"Now," said Smith, who had come to stand beside him. "We've established that you recognise the scene. So, tell me, do you recognise this man?"

It was the last thing that Jack had expected to be asked.

"No," he said, honestly. "I've never seen him before."

"Look closer," said Smith.

Jack did as he was asked. The man's face was so battered that it was barely recognisable as human, but as he stared at it, he suddenly realised who was hanging before him. But he needed to be sure.

"Can you turn him around?" he said to Smith. "I need to see his hands."

Smith said something in an unintelligible language and Balthazar stepped forward and used the curled up whip in his hand to prod the man's body until it spun on the rope holding it, giving Jack a view of the hands that were bound behind his back. Jack noticed the tell-tale tattoos on the man's fingers, and he knew who it was.

"It's the Russian," he said to Smith. "It's Boris Kerensky, the man I met in Marseilles. The man who had my colleague crucified," he added.

"You're absolutely sure?" said Smith.

"Yes, I'm sure. I wasn't at first, because his face is such a mess, but now I can tell that it is, and those weird tattoos on his fingers are a dead giveaway. That man is Boris Kerensky."

"Congratulations, Mr Mears," said the demon. "You have fulfilled your true function for the day. A job well done. Thank you."

"What do you mean?" said Jack, as they stepped back from the heat of the fire. "Is that the real reason you brought me all the way down here? Just to identify someone? Is that what this is really all about?"

"You must have guessed there was an ulterior motive. You don't really think I'd go to all the trouble of finding you and getting you down here, not to mention parting with a hundred thousand euros, just for you to give me a lift, do you? Mr Balthazar would very happily do that for me. The journey to the frontier was the cover; the money was the hook. In fact, you put up rather more resistance to the idea than I thought you might, given your precarious situation, but I'm glad to say I talked you round in the end."

"I didn't really feel I had a lot of choice," said Jack.

"Perhaps not. But you were nevertheless misled, and for that I offer my apologies. And as it happens, I do need to be taken to the frontier tonight, so this has been far from a wasted journey."

"So this was all about him?" said Jack, looking at the inert figure of the Russian called Kerensky, who appeared to have lapsed into unconsciousness, in spite of the flames licking at his head. "I don't understand."

"Of course you don't," said Smith, adopting a kindly, almost fatherly tone of voice. "I realise that you have been left rather in the dark about the events of today, so let me try and shed some light.

"Mr Kerensky is an erstwhile devotee of mine who I'm sorry to say abused my trust very badly, and who has caused me great displeasure. The various nuances of this matter are unimportant, but suffice to say, he is about to suffer rather terribly for his betrayal.

"The problem was identifying him. You see, I had never met this man until this evening. His services were engaged by another of my people, who Mr Kerensky had killed, and I simply had no idea what he looked like."

"I don't get it," said Jack. "You knew who I was. You know everything there is to know about me. How come you couldn't identify him?"

"Because Kerensky is a skilled adept in the occult arts, and as such was able to protect himself, up to a point; to cloak himself and keep out of my view, as it were. But on the night before you arrived in Toulouse he made a serious error by having your friend so gruesomely killed. His methodology was what gave him away; even the Russian underworld aren't quite that depraved.

"I have people working for me in many places, including the city of Marseilles, and the crime he committed was very quickly brought to my attention. I suspected it was Kerensky, and that he had revealed himself at last, but I couldn't be sure. So, Mr Balthazar and some colleagues picked him up, and took him to the house in the woods. That same day, I travelled to Toulouse to find you, Mr Balthazar having been advised that you were a former colleague of the man Kerensky killed, and next on his hit list. That part of what I told you was entirely true. In fact, it was only Balthazar's capture of Kerensky that prevented the Russians from getting to you in Toulouse, although you may be interested to know that they weren't far away by the time we left the city this afternoon. You're not that hard to find, Mr Mears.

"For me, of course, it was easy, given certain advantages I have, and so for the next few days I watched you as you came to that bar each afternoon, waiting futilely for the arrival of your colleague. I learned everything there was to know about you during this period; everything you've ever done, every thought you've ever had. That's something I can do. It's a gift I have.

"And then I made my approach," he finished.

"The once in a lifetime opportunity," Jack said softly.

"Yes. That was the bait, and knowing by then, as I did, the dire situation you were in, I was fairly confident that you would accept it. Eventually, you did."

"Why bother?" said Jack. "Why not just get Balthazar to snatch me off the street, like you did with Kerensky?"

"Please, Mr Mears," said Smith, sounding affronted. "Why on earth would I do such a thing? You were not my enemy, you had not wronged me in any way, or caused me displeasure of any kind. I should no more consider harming you without reason than I would any other person entirely innocent of this affair. Really, for someone with no religious beliefs whatsoever, you do have a most old fashioned and, if I may say, rather prejudiced view of my nature. Bringing you down here forcibly was only ever a last resort. It was always my wish that this could be accomplished in a civilised fashion.

"Besides," he added, almost as an afterthought, "After observing you for only a short time, I came to find you rather interesting, and so I decided to observe you for a little while longer."

Jack didn't like to think why that might be, but decided to let it pass.

"Seems like a long time to spend, just watching me," he muttered.

"When you have lived as long as I have," said Smith, "Time is something one has in abundance. My concept of its passage would be completely different to yours. There was no rush."

"So that's what all this was about?" Jack said, motioning around him at the castle walls, and the ghastly scene in front of them.

"Actually, no," said Smith. "This was very much a spur of the moment thing; prompted by you, I might add. You see, my original intention had been for you to make the identification back at the house, where Kerensky was being kept behind that locked door you seemed so interested in earlier this afternoon. We would then proceed to the frontier as planned, and I would pay you your money. But then you took such a keen interest in that book in the shop window, and on the way to visit Mr Balthazar, well, what can I say – the idea of re-creating the scene in the book simply fell into my head. I then suggested this to Mr Balthazar and we concocted our little scheme accordingly. But I never imagined he'd do such an exemplary job in setting this all up for our entertainment.

"Exemplary, Mr Balthazar, truly exemplary," he called out to the old man, who gave a guttural bark in response.

As he was saying this, Kerensky had regained consciousness, and he made a strangulated sound.

"I think he's trying to say something," said Smith.

"Please," croaked the man, in English. "Please don't do this."

"Good evening, Mr Kerensky," said Smith, walking over to the fire. "And so we finally meet. I have brought Mr Mears with me. You remember Mr Mears, don't you? You met him in Marseilles. Shortly before you had his colleague crucified."

"No," protested the Russian. "That was not me. You have the wrong man. Please … master," he added.

"Please, master," Smith echoed softly. "How the guilty repent. I'm sorry, Mr Kerensky, but we're well past that. When you so foolishly betrayed my trust, I ceased to be your master, and you, my servant. Now, you are my enemy, and you are going to suffer a very horrible punishment for having crossed me.

"*Pour encourager les autres*," he said to Jack.

"Mr Balthazar, the fire seems to have died a bit. Perhaps you should add a little more wood."

The old man made a giggling sound, and ran the back of his hand across his lips, before ducking behind a low wall and then re-emerging with a pile of kindling in his arms, which he started to place on the fire. The wood must have been dry, because it seemed to catch immediately, causing flames to leap from the fire into Kerensky's face, and Jack thought he heard the sound of hair singeing.

Smith turned and spoke softly to the woman and she stepped towards the fire. Just as she had that afternoon, when serving Jack his tea, she passed by him much closer than she needed to, and her hips brushed provocatively against him.

But Jack wasn't prepared for what she did next.

She shouted something at the man hanging above the flames, in the same sort of peculiar dialect that the old man had used, and which was more animal than human. And then, in one fluid movement, she drew the arm holding the spiked club back over her shoulder and swung it hard at the man's head. The club made a swishing noise as it passed through the air, and then wedged itself in the neck of the upside down man, who gave a shriek of pain.

Jack gasped at the brutal action of the woman, and it was all he could do not to run away. Only the knowledge of the consequences of such an action prevented him from doing so. He made a physical effort to hold himself to the spot and continue to stand there.

The woman pulled the club from the man's neck, and a jet of blood poured from the wound into the fire, causing the flames to hiss and spit.

Brushing close by Jack once again, and grinning at him from pouting lips, the woman went and resumed her place with the others.

The Russian must have known the game was up by then, because rather than continue to plead for his life, he started talking softly to himself; a dialogue interspersed with cries of pain every time the flames rose to meet his head and torso.

"What's he saying?" said Jack, after they had observed the foul scene for a while longer.

"I think he's trying to pray," said Smith, as if straining to hear.

"I suppose you could say," he continued, "That he is attempting to cover all his bases, before the end comes."

They stood there for several more moments, with Smith and his helpers apparently happy to watch the man suffer. Finally, Smith seemed to shake himself out of his grim reverie.

"Right, then," he said, all business again. "I think we have detained ourselves here for long enough, enjoyable though it's been. Time to deal with this and move on. The gun, please, Mr Balthazar."

The old man stepped over to Smith, and with a short bow, handed a pistol to him that Jack recognised as a snub nosed revolver.

At least we're getting it over with, he thought to himself, not anticipating what was to come next.

"Take it," ordered Smith, passing the gun to him.

"What …?" Jack began, as he felt the cold metal in his hand.

"Now, kill him," said Smith.

"What?" Jack repeated, aghast at the thought of shooting this poor wretch.

"You heard me. Kill him. Put a bullet into this vermin, and we can be away from here."

"No way," said Jack, summoning his last reserves of defiance. "I won't. I can't. I'm not going to shoot someone.

"Why don't you do it?" he tried, attempting to hand the gun to Smith.

"Because I asked you to," said Smith, coming over to Jack, so that their faces were just inches apart, and with his voice barely above a whisper and full of menace. "So stop embarrassing me in front of my friends and get on with it."

"But what about the sound of the gun?" Jack said, desperately trying to play for time. "Someone will hear it. Down in the village, someone will hear it."

"They'll hear it," said Smith. "They won't do anything about it?"

"Why not?"

"Because they know I'm up here."

There was nothing Jack could say to that. He knew that he'd run out of options. As much as he didn't want to shoot the man, he didn't seem to have any choice.

What difference did it make, he asked himself. If he didn't kill him then Smith or Balthazar would, so it was a moot point who pulled the trigger. Besides, the man was suffering terribly. It would be a mercy killing.

He looked round and saw Smith's three helpers, their hoods now removed, watching him expectantly.

"Do it," the woman hissed at him, before running her tongue lasciviously across her lips. Jack recalled the black lipstick she had been wearing that afternoon and for some reason he wondered if she was wearing it now. Her breasts hung pendulously above the folds of her cloak and Jack wondered if her nipples were smeared with lipstick too, making him feel aroused and disgusted in equal measure.

I really am losing it, he thought.

He raised the gun. It felt heavy in his hand. As he pointed it towards the man's suspended midriff he felt a bead of sweat run down his forehead and into his eyes and he wiped it away with the back of his other hand. Taking a deep breath he started to pull the trigger. It seemed to take an age. The last thing he saw before he felt the gun jerk in his hand and heard it's deafening retort echo around the mountain valley, was the wide-eyed, terrified, upside down stare of a man he had met once, a lifetime ago, and whose life he was about to extinguish, on the say-so of a demon and his gang of acolytes.

The bullet had hit Kerensky in the chest but it hadn't killed him. The gurgling sound he was making as his lungs filled with blood was proof of that. Jack heard someone, Balthazar he presumed, give a little squeal of delight. He looked around and saw the old man grinning at him.

"Finish it," he shouted, drawing his hand across his throat. It was the first time that Jack had heard him speak in English.

"Finish it," echoed the woman, pointing at Jack.

As she said this, the boy went and crouched by the fire, and stared with childlike inquisitiveness at the dying man. Jack looked for the snake he had previously been holding above his head and wondered where it had gone. And then he noticed something moving within the boy's cloak, and saw the serpent's head emerge from its hem.

Of course, Jack said to himself, his thoughts turning back to the scene in the book. The child in the picture had looked like it had a tail.

The snake finished uncoiling itself from the boy's cloak, dropped to the ground, and slithered away into the darkness.

The child continued to crouch by the fire, rocking lightly on his haunches, seemingly mesmerised by the scene of torture and death that he was witnessing. He was singing to himself, softly, under his breath, so that it was barely audible above the crackle of the fire and the death rattle gasps of the dying man, and in a language that Jack couldn't understand.

Then he stood up and walked over to Jack, looking up at him with pitiless, dead eyes.

"Finish it, Jack," he said.

Jack looked round for Smith, who had remained silent ever since the shot rang out. He was looking, not at Jack or at the condemned man, but at the boy. Pride and love were evident in his features.

Jack looked back at the Russian above the fire.

Just finish it, he said to himself.

He raised the gun again, pointed it at the man's chest, and pulled the trigger five times in quick succession, the recoil reverberating in his hand and up his arm, the sound deafening within the walled enclosure of the castle courtyard.

The man's body jerked on its rope and then was still. The sound of gunfire continued to echo for a time before eventually fading, and the air filled with the smell of cordite. And then all was strangely quiet, and even the wind seemed to drop for some reason, and all that could be heard was the crackle of the fire.

"Congratulations," Smith said, coming to stand beside Jack, who was continuing to stare at the body of the man he had just killed.

"It gets easier," he said as he took the gun from him and tossed it over to Balthazar, who caught it deftly and slipped it into the folds of his cloak.

"Well, it's done now," said Jack, trying to sound a lot more casual than he felt. Oddly enough, he didn't feel anything much at all, in that moment, just a strange feeling of emptiness.

"Best thing for him, really," he continued, for his own benefit, as much as anything. "At least he's not suffering any more."

"Actually," said Smith, "His suffering is only just beginning."

He went and stood by the fire and said something under his breath that Jack couldn't hear, and then turned back to face Jack and the others.

"Our work here is done," he said. "Thank you again, Mr Balthazar, for your most splendid efforts this evening."

Balthazar gave a courteous bow to his master and the woman and child followed suit, and Smith acknowledged this gesture by nodding back at them.

"Mr Mears?" he said, enquiringly. "Ready to go?"

"Eh?" said Jack, lost in thought as he stared at the dead man hanging above the fire.

"Are you ready? Midnight is approaching, and I still need to get to the frontier. That was the original deal, if you recall.

"Shall we?" he said, glancing towards the castle entrance.

"Whatever you say," Jack mumbled.

He gave a final wary look towards the three cloaked figures and turned to follow Smith.

"We shall leave the others to tidy up," said Smith as they walked out of the walled enclosure. "We can't have a group of tourists tripping over the unfortunate Mr Kerensky when they come up here in the morning, can we now?"

There was a jauntiness about him, Jack noticed, in the aftermath of the killing. It was as if he had a renewed spring in his step as he strode out of the castle.

And as they walked back down the stony path to the car park at the foot of the castle, Jack felt his own tension ebb away, and he was gripped instead by a feeling of relief and good humour that puzzled him. Was this merely the result of his having survived the trip up to the castle, he asked himself.

Smith, as ever, appeared to be reading his mind, and unsurprisingly he had a somewhat different explanation for Jack's improved mood.

"Feels good, doesn't it?" he said as they got to the car.

"What does?" said Jack.

"What you just did; exercising power in that way; holding a man's life, his very destiny, in your hands like that. It feels good, I can tell. Having been a fugitive for so long, having to kow-tow to the likes of that creature in there … well, demonstrating your mastery over him in the way that you just did, it must feel rather pleasing. Am I wrong?

"No," said Jack, shaking his head slowly at Smith over the roof of the car. "No, you're not wrong. It did feel good. It still does feel good. What does that say about me, I wonder?"

"That you're a man and not a worthless insect," said Smith. "Don't diminish the necessary task you just accomplished by allowing the weakness of your humanity to question it. Don't fight it. Embrace it."

Jack didn't think he wanted to go quite that far, but he wasn't in the mood to contradict a demon.

"So where to now?" he said, changing the subject as they got into the car. "Which way to the frontier?"

"Back through the village to the main road," said Smith as he settled himself into his seat. "I'll direct you from there."

Finally, the last leg of the journey, Jack thought to himself as they drove away from the castle. The moment I've been waiting for all day; the moment where Smith will either pay me what he owes me and walk away from my life forever, or else he'll enact whatever fiendish plan truly underpins his intentions on this day.

Smith, of course, could read these thoughts, a gift Jack was fervently hoping would lose its potency once he was no longer in close proximity to him, assuming such a happy turn of events ever came to pass.

"You have nothing whatsoever to fear from me," he said. "I know that it's been on your mind all day, but I can assure you that nothing is going to happen to you at the frontier. I've kept my word up to this point; perhaps it's time you trusted me a little more."

"You said I wouldn't have to kill anyone. Yesterday, at the bar, you said I wouldn't have to kill anyone."

"That's true," Smith conceded. "And at the time I spoke those words, it was certainly not my intention that you should do so. But this evening, having so carefully prepared that tableau for you, it seemed the most appropriate course of action. It was irresistible, really, given the circumstances, but I'm sorry if I misled you.

"Besides," he added softly, "It was important that I knew you could do something like that, if asked. I needed to know that, for my own reasons."

Jack decided not to dwell on why that might be and concentrated instead on driving the car.

They passed through the darkened village and got back onto the main road, and then a short distance later they reached the turn-off for the border with Spain, which Jack calculated was about an hour's drive away.

Smith had been silent since leaving the castle, save for pointing out the turning off the main road, and they didn't speak as they drove through the darkness into the mountains.

They travelled for a while along a slow, twisting road crowded on either side by thick woods, but the closer they got to the frontier, the more the terrain seemed to open out.

Jack took advantage of the straighter road to press down on the accelerator and increase their speed. The car seemed to purr beneath him as it sped towards their destination.

Nearly there, he thought to himself as they passed another sign pointing to the border ahead. Just keep going; you've almost made it.

But as he was thinking this, Smith spoke for what seemed like the first time in an age.

"There is a forest road off to the left," he said. "Just ahead of us. You need to take this turning. We're very close now, to the place we're going."

Jack slowed the car as they drew level with an un-signposted minor road that led into the woods, and felt a now familiar fear return as he came to a halt by the turning.

"Problem?" said Smith, taking a precautionary look behind him.

"What's down there?" said Jack. "The frontier is this way," he added, pointing down the road that stretched into the blackness ahead of them.

"No, actually it isn't," said Smith. "The border between France and Spain is that way. The frontier is this way," he said, pointing into the forest to their left.

"So the frontier isn't the same thing as the border?" said Jack.

"I never said it was."

"No, I suppose you didn't. What is it, then?"

"It's the place from which I return to my world."

"Your world."

"Yes."

"And it's down there?" Jack said dubiously, peering into the gloom of the forest.

"Just a few miles further down that road," said Smith.

With great reluctance, Jack steered the car onto the road and began to drive slowly into the woods. The road was completely straight and flanked on either side by tall firs, like a giant natural corridor.

Jack glanced anxiously into the rear view mirror out of a sudden fear that the pickup truck driven by Balthazar might have followed them here, and that Jack might be destined to suffer the same grisly fate as Kerensky, but the road was empty behind them, and it felt as if they had been swallowed up by the darkness on all sides.

On and on they continued down the seemingly endless forest road, with Jack waiting for some signal from Smith telling him to pull over. But such a sign never came. Instead, the road merely came to an end by some corrugated metal barns, open at the sides, and Jack stopped the car and switched off the engine.

He looked out into the darkness of the woods. They had stopped at what appeared to be some sort of logging station, now deserted and derelict.

"We walk from here," said Smith. "It's not far."

They got out of the car. Jack could hear the wind in the trees that towered above them. Smith retrieved his attaché case from the back and immediately set off down a grass track that led into the forest, and Jack fell into step behind him.

"To get back to the car," Smith said to Jack over his shoulder, "Merely follow this path, and you won't get lost."

"Right," said Jack, heartened by the suggestion that he would be returning this way later.

It was almost pitch dark under the dense cover of the trees and Jack could barely make out the path he was walking on. But Smith seemed to have an innate sense of where he was going, and was striding briskly ahead, much as he had on the way up to the stone chair that afternoon.

They walked for just a few minutes before coming to a clearing so large it was more like a field ringed by trees, and which seemed almost bathed in light compared to the darkness of the thick woods now behind them. Smith stopped at the edge of the tree line, and indicated that Jack should do the same.

"Is it here?" he asked.

"It's there," said Smith, pointing at the trees on the other side of the enclosure, and Jack saw a fire burning at the tree line. He could just make out the shape of two human figures standing beside it.

"So that's the frontier," said Jack.

"Yes, it is."

"What is it?"

"It's the place where I cross over to my world. It's really a doorway, or portal, one of a great many in this world, more than you could possibly imagine, and which open at set intervals, enabling those such as I to pass through them. The one you see over there has not opened in this spot for many hundreds of years, and after it has closed this evening, it will not open again for a similar length of time."

"Who are the two people standing next to it?" Jack asked.

"They guard the frontier," said Smith. "They are here to ensure that I pass through the portal without incident, and also to prevent unwanted incursions. Or excursions," he added.

Just a few short hours ago, Jack thought, a conversation such as this would have seemed utterly insane. Now, not so much.

"So that's it then," he said. "The end of the road."

It felt more like a hopeful question than a statement of fact.

"Yes," said Smith. "And quite a road it was that we travelled today, was it not, Mr Mears?"

"You can say that again."

Jack started to feel more at ease; started to allow himself to believe that he might be getting through this, after all.

Smith put his attaché case onto the trunk of a deadfall that lay across the edge of the clearing. The sound of it opening was loud in the still night air. He pulled out a thick envelope which he handed to Jack.

"Ninety thousand euros," he said. "The balance of what I owe you."

Jack opened the envelope, saw the thick wedge of banknotes, closed it again, and put it into the pocket of his jacket, which he zipped shut.

"Thank you," he said.

"Not at all," replied the demon. "You've earned it, I feel, given what has transpired today. The car is also yours to keep, or sell, as you wish."

Jack had wondered about that, indeed had wondered if Smith had intended to drive off in it at the so-called frontier, before Jack knew what this was, leaving him to walk back through the forest to goodness knows where. Smith's gift of the car was welcome news. Jack would sell it as soon as he got to a large town, swap it for something smaller and less conspicuous, and add the change left over to his newly acquired wealth.

"Thanks," he said. "Nice bonus. That guy in Toulouse isn't expecting it back, then?"

"No," said Smith. "He passed away, you see, earlier this evening."

Jack's heart gave a now familiar skip as he recalled the frightened little man in the garage forecourt.

"How unfortunate," he said casually, trying to keep it cool. "Anyway, I'd best be off. Follow the track, right? So, thanks again, Mr Smith, for the … you know … the opportunity. I guess my employment is at an end."

Smith looked at him for a long moment.

"If you wish it to be," he said.

"I don't follow," said Jack.

Smith glanced over at the fire on the other side of the clearing.

"We still have some time, before I need to cross over. Let's sit for a while." He motioned towards the fallen tree trunk.

The last thing Jack wanted to do was spend a moment more in that forest than he had to, but feeling he couldn't really refuse, he went and sat down by the demon.

"It really is a very beautiful spot, isn't it?" he said to Jack. "In the daytime, you can see the tops of the mountains beyond the trees. I have a great fondness for this place, for this whole region. In so many ways, it reminds me of home.

"You find that hard to believe," he said, accurately reading Jack's thoughts. "Do you really think my world is as it's described in the Bible – some phantasmagorical, burning landscape, set beneath eternal darkness, and populated by the damned? It's nothing like that. It's much more like this; more vivid, perhaps, more fantastic in its way, but physically, not so very different.

"Perhaps that is why I have always felt so comfortable here, in these valleys and mountains.

"This is where I found Mr Balthazar. It was in a town not far from here, several centuries ago, during the time of the Inquisition. He was being tortured to death by some zealous Christians who had charged him with dabbling in the occult. Little did they know. Mr Balthazar was in fact a most skilful practitioner of the dark arts, even then, and a devotee of mine of many years standing.

"I watched the Christian soldiers flay the skin from his body, while the supine townsfolk built the funeral pyre to place him on. Never was a man so doomed, and yet the defiance he showed that night, the contempt that shone in his eyes for those soldiers of the Christian god, and for the priests, those hideous black crows with their pious sermons and homilies – it was a magnificent sight. I knew, as I watched from the baying crowd, that I could not allow such a beautiful creature to be destroyed, and that I would offer him immortality in return for his devoted service.

"I killed many men that night, freeing him, and afterwards I reduced the whole town to ash. I am very loyal, you see, to those who serve me, just as I am merciless towards those who defy me."

"So Mr Balthazar is hundreds of years old?" Jack said, less incredulously than he would have done a day previously.

"I suppose you could say that he is," said Smith, "Except, once transformed like that, there is no longer any such concept as old. One just is."

"And the woman is … his wife?" Jack asked.

"His daughter. The boy is his grandson. I'm so very proud of them all; they are truly like family to me."

"So," he said, after they had sat silently for a few moments, listening to the wind in the trees, "What is next for you, Mr Mears, after you leave this forest tonight?"

"I haven't thought too much about it," Jack replied. "To be honest with you, Mr Smith, all I've really cared about up to now was just getting through today."

"That's understandable. But I suppose you could say that almost every day is a bit like that for you; a question of survival, of getting through it, as you put it, of evading capture or death from those who pursue you, merely surviving to live another day. Is today really all that different from any other?"

"It is now," Jack said with a grin, patting the bulky envelope in his pocket.

"It is for now," Smith said in response. "The money has brought you some time, I grant you. It's given you some breathing space, some temporary respite for as long as you can stay alive. But in the great scheme of things, is it really going to make all that much difference?

"Let me see if I can predict how things will go for you, having left me in this forest. You'll drive away from here with that fat envelope in your pocket, and you'll find somewhere to lie low for a while, in order to evade the Russians and the various other furies pursuing you, and you'll enjoy a little downtime. Am I correct so far?"

"Sounds good to me," said Jack.

"Doubtless it does, given the straitened circumstances in which I found you. So let's jump forward a bit. Of course, you'll enjoy your newly earned riches for a while, so much so that you'll spend more of it than you intend. And then what? That money won't last forever, maybe won't last much more than a year, given that you're on the run, so what happens next?

"France doesn't seem to be the answer for you. Aside from your inability to speak the language, you have no useful contacts here, now that your associate is dead, and the respective criminal gangs of which he and the recently departed Mr Kerensky were members will still be looking for you. That said – and herein lies the catch for you, I suppose – the greatest advantage to your staying in this country is the fact that, being wanted by the authorities as you are, leaving it might be problematic. You could assume a new identity, of course, change your appearance, purchase the necessary papers, but that would eat quite considerably into your capital.

"And what would it really gain you? What would you do? Where would you go? Back to Spain? There's nothing for you there now, given the demise of your former employer, and we both know that it was only because of him that you were able to prosper there as you did; something you quickly discovered for yourself following his death. Without him, you're nothing in that country.

"I suppose you could return home to England, but that's not much of an option either, after you so impetuously skipped bail to go and join your cellmate in Spain. That hasn't been forgotten in the interim. You're still very much a wanted man in your own homeland.

"And in any case, regardless of the various warrants you have against your name, it's the criminal fraternity you need to be most worried about.

"Particularly the colleagues of the man you killed tonight," he added. "They were out for your blood before. Imagine how keen they're going to be to catch up with you now. Well, I'm sure you don't need me to spell it out for you.

"So what are you to do? I'm sorry, Mr Mears, I don't mean to rain on your parade, but even with that princely sum in your pocket, you seem to have very few options. Of course, you'll enjoy spending the money while you still have plenty of it, but I see nothing good in your future, just pursuit by various state agencies, pursuit by other criminals, penury and eventually death or incarceration."

"You know all that for a fact?" Jack asked.

"No, I don't know any of it," said Smith. "Even I can't predict the future. Nobody can. I'm merely speculating."

"Well, I've never really thought too much about the future," Jack said as the euphoria of getting the money faded.

"Perhaps you should have," said Smith. "But what's done is done; we are where we are. The question is what to do now."

"Presumably, you have something in mind."

"I do, as it happens. I'm going to make you an offer."

"Make me an offer?"

"Yes. I'm going to offer you a once in a lifetime opportunity."

"Hold on," said Jack. "I thought you already did that. I thought that's what today was all about – my once in a lifetime opportunity."

"It is what today was all about. The chance to earn one hundred thousand euros for one day's work was indeed a once in a lifetime opportunity. However, I am about to offer you another one; a better one."

"Go on," said Jack.

"It's really quite simple," said Smith. "Join me. Come with me tonight. Come with me across the frontier."

Jack was speechless.

"You're not serious?" he finally managed to say.

"Do you really think I'd joke about such a thing?"

"No," Jack said. "I don't suppose you would. But I don't understand … If I came with you … What would happen?"

"You would serve me."

"How?"

"By being a highly valued emissary and enforcer. And you would spend much of your time here. You would be one of my right-hand men, my vicar on earth, if you'll excuse the pun, crossing back and forth through these portals, attending to my needs."

"So I'd be like Mr Balthazar."

"In certain respects. I might get him to mentor you. For the first couple of decades. Show you the ropes."

Jack let this sink in for a moment.

"Would I be selling my soul?" he asked after a few moments.

"That's a Christian notion that has no meaning to me," said Smith. "You'd be pledging your service to me, your fealty, for all eternity."

"For all eternity," Jack repeated.

"Yes, and in return, you would be rich and powerful beyond your wildest dreams."

Jack didn't know whether to feel flattered or terrified by Smith's offer. It was mind boggling; horrifying and yet alluring at the same time.

"No," he said finally. "I can't. It's not what I want. I've made some good money tonight. I'll use it to make a fresh start."

The demon shook his head.

"I'm sorry, Mr Mears, but what sort of fresh start do you really think is available to you, even with the money I've just given you? What are you going to do? Get a regular job? Start a small business? You're a wanted man, with the Russian mob, and goodness knows who else out for your blood. Such an option hasn't existed for you in a very long time. You long ago forfeited your opportunity to live a normal life."

"Then I'll go back to what I was doing before," Jack said defensively. "I'll get back in the drug business. I know how to do that. I have the funds now to go it alone, without having to bother about people like Henri."

"But Mr Mears, there is no going it alone in your line of work. You may have funds, but you'll still need contacts, suppliers, couriers, middle men, customers, and how long is it going to be before one of them lets you down again, just as they've been letting you down all your life?"

"How do you mean?" said Jack.

"While I was watching you in that bar in Toulouse, I learned a lot about you; everything there is to know, you might say. Your whole life, you've been undermined by those who are less intelligent and resourceful than you are. You may think that your associate in Marseilles was a particular kind of idiot, and he was. The most imaginative thing he ever did was getting himself crucified. But they've all been idiots. Like your accomplice you robbed a post office with, the job you went to prison for. A dolt if ever there was one – it would have been better for the world by far if the police had shot him dead that day. Even Bob Stern, your erstwhile employer in Spain, was a dullard in comparison to you; a timid creature with no ambition. You know all of this; you don't need me to tell you. All those thoughts passed through your head repeatedly during those hours you were waiting in that bar. You need to put those sort of people behind you, once and for all. Only I can help you to achieve your true potential, and believe me, Jack, you have so much potential."

It was the first time he had addressed Jack by his first name.

"I'm sorry, but no," said Jack. "I hear what you're saying, believe me I do, but your life, your world, what you do – it's not for me. I don't have it in me to be like you and Mr Balthazar. I'm just not like that."

"Oh, but I think we both know that you are exactly like that," said Smith. "You see, when I was delving into your subconscious, I went right back to the beginning. I'm aware of every bad thing you've ever done, every crime you've ever committed, every shameful and depraved thought you've ever had. Why else do you think I'd want to recruit you so much that I'd make you an offer like this?

"I was there when you stole your first car – the same model as the one I got you to drive today, in the hope that it would jog your memory. I was there when you carried out your first armed robbery, when you first peddled drugs, when you first demanded protection. I was there for all of it.

"I saw what you did to that hapless shopkeeper, by the way, the one who wouldn't pay up. I saw the way you beat him, the pleasure you took in it."

"You saw that?" said Jack, recalling the incident from long ago.

"I saw much more than that. I saw the first child you bullied at school. I was there the first day you stole from a shop. I saw the girl who lived in your street, who thought the world of you, and who you so cruelly took advantage of. And I saw the tramp you kicked half to death, on your way home one night. Why did you do that? He was just a harmless derelict.

"Because you despised him," Smith answered for him. "Because you knew you were better than him; because you knew that you could; because you wanted to. Am I wrong?"

"No," Jack said softly, remembering. "You're not wrong."

"I've seen it all," Smith continued. "I saw the whore whose arm you broke when she couldn't pay for the drugs you'd procured for her. I saw the old lady, your parents' next door neighbour, whose life savings you stole, even though she had never shown you anything but kindness. And I saw the drug dealer you double crossed in Malaga, one of the ones you were working with on the side, without the knowledge of your employer, and who died because of what you did."

"I didn't know that," said Jack. "I didn't know that he'd died."

"Well, now you do. And he's not the only person who's been killed because of you in recent times, is he?"

Jack knew what was coming next.

"Bob Stern," he said. "You know about that as well, then?"

"Of course I do," said the demon. "That man took you in when you had nothing, treated you like a brother, and then you rather cleverly planted a false story about him with his associates in Morocco, suggesting he was a police informer, which you knew would get him killed. And all in the hope that you could move in and take over his business.

"It was a nice play, Jack, but that didn't work out for you either, did it? In fact, one could say that it backfired quite spectacularly, given that you failed to take over the man's business, and what was left of it no longer wanted to employ you."

"Look," said Jack, "Bob Stern may have been good to me in the past, he may have treated me like a brother to begin with, but by the end he was treating me like one of his kids. He treated me with contempt. Sure, I made that call, and I knew it would get him killed, but I did what I had to do."

"But Jack," said Smith, "I'm not judging you. I don't have the slightest problem with what you did. I approve of what you did. The man was holding you back, anyone could see that. I'm just sorry it didn't go to plan for you.

"But it was part of the reason I got you to pull that trigger, earlier this evening, in order to despatch the unfortunate Mr Kerensky. I needed to be sure that you could kill for yourself, rather than relying on others to do it for you, and happily you passed the test. Never employ a person unwilling to do their own dirty work. It's long been an adage of mine."

"Well, I'm glad I pleased you," Jack said, "But I still don't want to come with you."

"The choice, of course, is yours," said the demon. "But I would most strongly urge you to reconsider. There's nothing for you here, Jack; there hasn't been for a very long time. Staying here, in the final analysis, gains you nothing. Coming with me; well, it gains you everything.

"Besides, I don't mean to accentuate the negative, but if we're talking incentives, it's not going to be long before the Russians have people all over the south of France, looking for you. And they'll keep looking, Jack, wherever you run to. Because these people never forget. And then it's just a matter of time. And you know they're really going to go to work on you, don't you, Jack? I mean, after what happened up at that castle tonight, they're going to have to make an example of someone. So you could say, I'm your one and only chance of salvation."

"You told me to do it," said Jack, with anger in his voice. "You told me to kill him. I'm much more implicated in all of this than I ever was before. And it's mostly thanks to you."

"What can I say?" Smith said with a shrug. "I like to stack the odds in my favour, in order to get what I want, and I want you, Jack. And I'm still your best chance of salvation, regardless of how we got here.

"But this is about much more than salvation; it's about much more than mere sanctuary from your various pursuers. It's about a whole new opportunity for you.

"Imagine a world where you would be answerable only to me, where you'd never have to run away from anything, ever again, and where it would be you who'd have the power, and where people would run from you. Imagine a world where nothing would be denied to you, and where you would be able to satisfy every desire, every perverted fantasy, every violent impulse that you have ever had. Imagine a world where you would no longer have to fear those like the man you killed tonight, and where, if you wanted, you could wrap a pathetic wretch like that in chains and ride him like a mule. Imagine that, Jack. Imagine being able to do everything you ever wanted. Without consequences.

"Come and join us. We are the Fallen, but the time is coming when we will rise again. Look at the world around you. Look at the death and misery and despair that prevails. This is our time, Jack, the time when we shall reclaim what is rightfully ours, and you could be sat at my right hand while we do it. Join us. All you have to do is walk across that clearing, towards the fire."

"And if I don't?" Jack said.

"Then we'll never see each other again," said the demon. "On that, you have my solemn word. This is all about free will, Jack. It doesn't work any other way."

He picked up his case and glanced across the field.

"I should get going," he said. "I'll leave you to make your decision. You still have a few minutes left, but when that fire goes out, the portal will have closed."

"I'll think about it," Jack whispered, to himself as much as to the entity who called himself Smith.

"I almost forgot your book," said the demon. He opened the attaché case and pulled out the book bearing the image that Jack would forever more associate in his mind with killing a man above a fire in a castle courtyard, and handed it to him.

"You left it behind," he said, "In all the excitement up at the castle. Should you decide to cross over with me, be sure to bring it with you. We can study it together.

"Well, I shall leave you now. Thank you most sincerely, Jack, for your service today. It's been quite an experience for both of us, and I shall remember our time together fondly. Good luck to you."

Jack watched the demon walk away from him towards the fire. When he got about half-way across the small field he stopped, and turned back to face him. For a long moment he just stood there, and then he slowly raised his arm in salutation before turning away. Jack saw him reach the flames, where he stopped briefly beside the two wraith-like figures who guarded the portal, and then he moved into the woods and was swallowed up by the darkness.

With a resigned and exhausted feeling, Jack stared across at the fire.

After a few moments, as he had known that he would, he started to walk towards it.

When he was just a short distance away, he stopped. He looked up at the night sky, and at the jagged line of tree tops, and felt the cool, pine scented breeze on his face.

Everything in the world suddenly seemed so beautiful. It was such a perfect night. If only things could have been different, he thought. If only everything could have been different. If only he could have been different. If only he could start all over again.

He let his eyes drift down the high wall of trees and saw the men by the fire, silently watching him. He was close enough to hear the crackle of the flames.

I wish it all could have been different, Jack thought again. He knew he was a bad person; he knew he was worse than a bad person; he knew he had done terrible things and the demon had been right in everything it had said. Never before had Jack's whole miserable existence been more vividly or succinctly described to him.

It had taken the words of a demon to show Jack who he truly was, but in that instant he realised that, by doing so, the demon had shown Jack what he had to do.

He could never make up for what he had done in the past. He would never be able to find that sort of redemption, any more than he could evade indefinitely those who pursued him and who, for all Jack knew were closing in on this place in the forest at that very moment. He knew all of this.

But for the first time in his life, thanks to the self-knowledge the demon had chosen to give him, and thanks to the bulky envelope full of cash now in his possession, he could at least try, in whatever brief time he had left, to make amends. He could do something, some small thing that was good, before the Russians eventually found him.

Standing there, just yards from the gateway to hell, Jack experienced a moment of epiphany. He had stared into the abyss, and everything had suddenly become clear to him – what he was, and what he had done.

And what he now had to do.

Dropping the book to the ground he turned away from the fire and walked swiftly back to the other side of the clearing. When he reached the tree line he turned around and saw that the fire was still burning, but more faintly than it had been before. And then, as he watched, it disappeared completely, and all was darkness again.

Feeling a sense of purpose and contentment that he had never before known, Jack set off into the forest.

It was time to do something good with his life.

THE END

COMING SOON

THE GATES OF WALPURGIS

A NOVEL BY

RICHARD WEBSTER

Richard and Alan had been best friends at university, inseparable comrades in arms. Then over the course of the next twenty years, they drifted apart. Richard went first into journalism, and then tried to become a novelist, whilst Alan enjoyed huge success as the front man for a rock band, and then retired with his riches to the depths of the Wiltshire countryside, near to the ancient megalithic site of Avebury, in a house once owned by Dorian Slake, a notorious occultist of the 1960s.

So when an impromptu reunion brings the two friends together again, Richard couldn't be more pleased, and when Alan offers him the chance to look after his country retreat, so that he can finish his book, things appear truly serendipitous.

But from the moment of his arrival at the isolated farmhouse, Richard starts to realize that all is not as it seems. Strange phenomena afflict the house with frightening regularity, and someone appears to be keeping watch on it from some nearby woods. Why is it that a local coven of Satanists seem to take such an inordinate interest in the property, mounting a campaign of harassment to force Richard to leave? And can there be any truth to the rumour that the Neolithic burial mound at the end of the garden conceals a Satanic temple beneath?

Desperate for answers, and with his friend having disappeared, Richard enlists the help of a local archaeologist, and an elderly expert in the occult, who once fought his own lonely battle against the Satanist, Dorian Slake. And so begins a terrifying race against time to uncover the hideous secret that lies beneath the burial mound, and to prevent Slake's diabolical plan, decades in the making, from wreaking a devastating calamity upon the world.

DUE FOR RELEASE IN DECEMBER 2024